在全球化的商業趨勢下

晉升經理人必備英語專書

張文娟 著

經理人英文
English For Managers
商業管理英語需知

五南圖書出版公司 印行

Preface

This is a book on business management English, written particularly for managers and others who are interested in broadening their knowledge of business English. The book is comprised of seven chapters of different important topics, and each has several units. In Chapters 1 - 6, every unit is made up of four sections: Dialogue, Article, Terminology and Famous quotes. The last chapter has five case studies of successful enterprises. The aim of the book is to aid readers in their studies of English for business purposes. While studying the book, please listen to the recording at the same time to gain familiarity with its content. If you find any inaccuracy in this book, please point it out, so that it may be included at the time of revision. Thank you very much.

Wen-chuan Chang

My special thanks go to my family, especially my parents, and my friends: Jia-Ying Wen, Justin Chen and Laura Carter. Also, I'd like to thank MBAlib (http://wiki.mbalib.com/) and Wikipedia (http://www.wikipedia.org/) for the valuable information they provided.

前　言 .....

　　這是一本關於商業管理英文的專書，特別是為了經理人和想要增進商用英語知識的人而寫的。本書分為七章，各有不同的重要主題，每章有數個單元，第一章至第六章的各單元由四個部分所組成：實境對話、文章、財經專業術語、名人語錄，最後一章為五個成功企業的個案研究。本書的目的是為了幫助讀者進修商業用途的英文，在研讀本書時，請同時聆聽課文錄音以更加深對書中內容的熟悉度。如果發現內容有任何錯誤之處，尚祈不吝指正，以利於修訂時納入改正。非常感謝！

張文娟

　　特別於此感謝我的家人，尤其是我的父母，還有我的友人：文家楹、陳家碉、Laura Carter，也要感謝 MBA 智庫百科（http://wiki.mbalib.com/）與維基百科（http://www.wikipedia.org/）所提供的寶貴資料。

contents
目錄

Chapter 1　Global Business Trends
全球商業趨勢

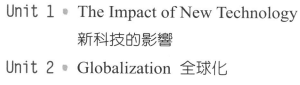

Unit 1 The Impact of New Technology
新科技的影響

1. Dialogue 實境對話

 1-1

A: Some friends of mine advised me to use social media in marketing. Do you know what that is?

B: Of course. It is a very powerful tool. People who want to promote a business, an organization or a foundation will find social media particularly useful.

A: Really? Can you give me some examples?

B: One of the most successful examples would be Apple. Hundreds and thousands of customers interact with the company via social media on a daily basis.

A: What makes Apple consumers want to do this?

B: Apple fans follow the updates of the company via social media and get a sense of belonging.

A: Now I can see why they become such loyal customers.

B: This is called "Bottom-up Communication," in contrast to the traditional "Top-down Communication." That's why interactivity is always emphasized in social media.

A: What you just mentioned is a big international tech company. I am just a small business owner who looks for strategies to navigate the increasingly complicated Internet.

B: Even I use Facebook to promote myself. We can surely find many creative ways of promoting the image of our company and marketing our business online by using social media.

A: Since you know so much about it, I'll assign this social media project to you. By this time next Monday, I'd like to see the established presence of our company on social media.

中文翻譯

A： 有一些朋友建議我用社群網站行銷，你知道那是什麼嗎？

B： 當然知道，社群網站這個工具非常有效，想要宣傳企業、組織、基金會的人特別會覺得社群網站極為有用。

A： 真的嗎？你可以舉例說明嗎？

B： 蘋果公司便是最成功的例子之一，成千上萬的顧客天天上社群網站來跟蘋果公司互動。

A： 為什麼蘋果公司的顧客要這麼做？

B： 果迷用社群網站追蹤公司最新動態，從中得到一種歸屬感。

A： 現在我明白他們為什麼會變成如此忠心的顧客。

B： 這叫作「由下而上的溝通」，有別於傳統的「由上而下的溝通」，這就是為什麼社群網站總是特別強調互動性。

A： 你剛所談的是個大型的跨國科技公司，而我只是個小型公司的老闆，在日益複雜的網路中努力尋找對策。

B： 連我也用臉書來自我行銷，我們一定可以用社群網站找到宣傳公司形象和行銷業務的方法。

A： 既然你對此了解如此深入，那麼我就將社群網站的企劃案交給你，到下星期一的這個時間，我就要看到我們公司在社群網站上成立好的樣子。

字彙與片語

- hundreds and thousands 成千上萬
- on a daily basis 每日
- a sense of belonging 歸屬感
- strategy ['strætədʒɪ] n. 策略
- assign [ə'saɪn] v. 委託
- establish [ə'stæblɪʃ] v. 成立

2. Article 文章

The Impact of New Technology on Business Management

New technology has revolutionized the current ways of managing a business, whether it is a small or medium-size business. Before investing much time and money to advance your technological equipment, it is wise to think about the pros and cons of employing certain new information technology in your businesses.

One of the new technological inventions many companies very find useful is social media. In the process of recruitment, the Human Resources Officers nowadays will look for potential new employees on websites for professionals. Increasingly, more and more companies use various social media for sales campaigns and public relations. Often customers can voice their feedback on a company's website, and their requests or complaints can be replied to online in an instant. Many non-governmental organizations (NGOs) make good use of the Internet to make the public aware of certain public issues and to encourage them to make contributions.

New information technology brings along with it some disadvantages as well. Communication software makes exchanging messages from a smartphone easier and faster than ever, but quite a few employees have complained about receiving instant messages after work hours or even being asked to work overtime. Furthermore, many information technology specialists find it hard to constantly deal with cyber security and hackers' attacks. Any data leaks of confidential files can be disastrous, and customers are wary of losing their personal data as a result. Even in online shopping, customers are worried that they will lose ownership of their data once they submit them to companies or that their data will be sold without their permission. The introduction of the Big Data has caused many people to be concerned about privacy issues.

In conclusion, striking a balance between the advantages and disadvantages of using new technology has become a great challenge for business managers in the modern competitive business world.

新科技對商業管理的影響

新科技對於現今企業管理的方法產生革命性的影響，無論是小型或中型企業。在你投資大量時間和金錢來更新科技設備前，可要多考量在你的企業使用某些新資訊科技的利與弊，才是明智之舉。

許多公司認為社群媒體是很有用的一項新科技發明，在雇用新人的過程中，人事部門長官現在會在專業人士的網站上尋找可能的新員工，越來越多的公司使用各種的社群媒體來進行銷售活動和公關活動，消費者經常可以在公司網站上表達他們的意見，他們的要求和抱怨可以馬上在網路上獲得回覆。很多非政府組織善用網路來讓大眾了解某些大眾議題，並鼓勵他們對此做貢獻。

新科技也帶來了壞處，通訊軟體使得用智慧型手機交換訊息變得很容易，很快速，但是很多員工抱怨在下班後收到即時訊息，或甚至被要求加班。還有，很多資訊科技人員常常感到網路安全和駭客入侵問題很難處理。任何機密資料的外洩都可能會有很悲慘的下場，客戶會擔心個人資料因此而外流。甚至在網路購物時，消費者憂心上傳個資給公司之後，他們將失去擁有個人資料的自主權，還有，他們的個資會不會不經過同意被賣給別人。大數據引進使得很多人擔心隱私權的問題。

總而言之，如何在使用新科技的優點和缺點中取得一個平衡點，成為了商業管理者在現代競爭激烈的商業世界中很大的挑戰。

- revolutionize [ˌrɛvəˈluʃənˌaɪz] v. 徹底改革

- the pros and cons 贊成和反對的理由

- leak [lik] n. （祕密等的）洩漏

- confidential [ˌkɑnfəˈdɛnʃəl] a. 祕密的；機密的

- disastrous [dɪzˈæstrəs] a. 災難性的，悲慘的

3. Terminology 財經專業術語

social media　社群網站

社群網站是一種網絡服務網站，即社會性網絡服務，目的在幫助人們建立社會性網絡的網路應用服務。網路社群的成員彼此不需面對面接觸，主要以電腦網路作爲互動的介面，藉著專屬的社群網站在網路上進行溝通、資訊分享、商品交易等互動。

marketing　行銷

行銷是指根據商品或服務的特點來規劃各種銷售策略及手段，以提升消費者的購買欲望，促進銷售量。

Top-down Communication　由上而下的溝通

由上而下的溝通就是指上級作爲訊息發佈者對下屬進行的一種溝通形式，這種縱向溝通是大部分傳統公司的溝通方式。

Bottom-up Communication　由下而上的溝通

由下而上的溝通是指下級向上級反映意見，以獲得一條讓管理者聽取員工或消費者意見的管道。

4. Famous Quotes 名人語錄

The PC has improved the world in just about every area you can think of. Amazing developments in communications, collaboration and efficiencies. New kinds of entertainment and social media. Access to information and the ability to give a voice to people who would never have been heard.

Bill Gates

個人電腦帶給這個世界各領域全面的進步，舉凡通訊、合作、效率方面都有驚人的發展，加上各式各樣的娛樂和社群網站，資訊的獲取變得更爲方便，而從前無法發表意見的人也都能藉此獲得發言權。

比爾・蓋茲

．．

Software innovation, like almost every other kind of innovation, requires the ability to collaborate and share ideas with other people, and to sit down and talk with customers and get their feedback and understand their Needs.

Bill Gates

軟體創新就像其他所有的創新一樣，需要具備與人合作的能力，與他人分享點子，與顧客坐下來討論，聆聽他們的回饋，並且明白他們的需要。

比爾・蓋茲

．．

Information technology and business are becoming inextricably interwoven. I don't think anybody can talk meaningfully about one without the talking about the other.

Bill Gates

資訊科技和商業漸漸變得密不可分，我認爲沒有人能夠真正將這兩者分開來談。

比爾 · 蓋茲

．．．

When you give everyone a voice and give people power, the system usually ends up in a really good place. So, what we view our role as, is giving people that power.

Mark Zuckerberg

給每個人發言權，讓大家都獲得權力，這樣的結果通常會讓整個系統都獲益，所以，我們認爲我們所該扮演的角色就是賦予所有人這種權力。

馬克 · 祖克柏

．．．

By giving people the power to share, we're making the world more transparent.

Mark Zuckerberg

藉由賦予大家這種一起分享的權力，我們讓這個世界漸漸變得更透明。

馬克 · 祖克柏

Unit 2　Globalization 全球化

1. Dialogue 實境對話　♪ 1-2

A: What's your final decision on working in China?

B: My wife hasn't approved of it yet.

A: Remember you only have three more days to consider it.

B: You really know how to put me in a dilemma. Are you saying if I don't agree to go, I'll be demoted?

A: That's basically the case. Anyway, you can visit your family in Taiwan every three months.

B: But my two kids are still quite small.

A: We need you to take charge of the factory in Dongguan now.

B: Why don't you send Kevin there?

A: Kevin is not capable of managing local Chinese workers.

B: Why is that?

A: He is simply not tough enough.

B: But I've never worked overseas so far in my whole life!

A: Don't worry. I can see you've got what it takes.

B: You are just saying so because you want to talk me into taking up the post.

A: Think about the high monthly pay.

B:　I know the salary is really attractive.
A:　You can take it as the advantage of globalization and capitalize on it.

中文翻譯

A：　你最後決定要去中國工作了嗎？

B：　我太太還沒有同意。

A：　要記得你只有三天可以考慮。

B：　你真叫我進退兩難，你的意思是說，如果我不同意去，就會被降職嗎？

A：　基本上就是如此。不管怎麼樣，你每三個月可以回台灣看家人一次。

B：　但是我的兩個小孩都還很小。

A：　我們現在需要你來管理東莞的工廠。

B：　為什麼不派凱文去那裡呢？

A：　凱文不知道如何管理當地中國工人。

B：　為什麼呢？

A：　他就是不夠強悍。

B：　不過我之前從來沒有在海外工作過！

A：　沒關係，我看得出來你有這個本事。

B：　你這麼說只是為了要說服我接下這個職位。

A：　想想每個月的高薪。

B：　我知道薪水非常吸引人。

A： 你可以把這個機會視為全球化所帶來的好處，好好從中獲利。

字彙與片語

- approve [ə'pruv] v. 同意；贊許
- dilemma [də'lɛmə] n. 困境，進退兩難
- demote [dɪ'mot] v. 降職
- post [post] n. 職位
- globalization [ˌgləʊbəlaɪ'zeɪʃən] n. 全球化
- capitalize ['kæpət!ˌaɪz] v. 利用

2. Article 文章

The Pros and Cons of Globalization

Globalization has been around in the world for quite a while, and most of us have been influenced by its practices without thinking too much about it. It has both positive and negative effects on us regardless of where we live.

Those who support globalization would argue that because of globalization, developed countries can purchase goods at a low price while people in developing countries can gain more work opportunities. Not only that, but outsourcing jobs to poor countries can stimulate the local economy and help emerging markets grow. Increasingly, consumers have access to products from different countries and this drives competition among manufacturers and corporations worldwide.

There are also downsides associated with globalization. Offshore outsourcing takes away the employment opportunities in the home country, and ideas of innovation could be easily stolen or copied by others. Quite a few tragic accidents among exploited laborers have been reported in the sweat shops in poor countries. Moreover, many multinational companies have gained political power and have become involved in various scandals.

Whether you like it or not, globalization only seems to be expanding to more parts of the world, not diminishing. While we consider its advantages and its disadvantages, it is hoped that we can achieve a win-win situation for ourselves in the wave of globalization.

全球化之利弊

全球化在世界上行之已久，我們大多數的人受到全球化影響而不自知，無論我們住在何處，全球化對我們產生的影響，包含有正面的與負面的。

支持全球化的人會說，因為全球化，已開發國家能以低價購買產品，而開發中國家的人能獲得更多的工作機會，不只這樣，將工作外包給貧窮的國家能夠刺激當地的經濟，幫助新興國家成長。消費者能有越來越多機會，選擇不同國家的產品，帶動了全世界製造商與企業的競爭。

全球化也產生了不利影響，離岸外包會減少國內的工作機會，而且創新點子可能會輕易被竊取或複製：在貧窮國家中，很多血汗工廠的勞工被剝削的悲劇頻傳。除此之外，很多跨國公司取得了政治權力，涉入各種醜聞。

不論你喜歡與否，全球化似乎只會擴張到世界更多地方，而不會減退，我們考慮全球化的優點與缺點時，希望我們能夠於這波全球化浪潮中，為自己爭取到雙贏結局。

- outsource [ˈaʊtsɔrs] v. 將……外包
- stimulate [ˈstɪmjəˌlet] v. 刺激；激勵
- downside [ˈdaʊnˈsaɪd] n. 缺點；不利
- offshore [ˈɔfˈʃor] a. 離岸的
- exploit [ɪkˈsplɔɪt] v. 剝削
- scandal [ˈskænd!] n. 醜聞
- diminish [dəˈmɪnɪʃ] v. 減少

3. Terminology 財經專業術語

☕ outsourcing　外包

　　外包為於 1980 年代流行起來的商業用語，是商業活動決策之一，指將承包合約之一部或甚至全部，委託或發交給承包合約當事人以外的第三人，以節省成本，集中精力於核心業務，善用資源，或為獲得獨立與專業人士的專業服務等等。

☕ value chain　價值鍊

　　價值鍊由波特（Michael Porter）於 1985 年所提出，在《競爭優勢》一書中，他指出企業如果要發展其獨特的競爭優勢，或為股東創造更高附加價值，就要將企業的經營流程解構成一系列的價值創造過程，而此價值流程的連結即是價值鍊。

trade agreement　貿易協定

貿易協定是指兩個或兩個以上的國家之間調整他們相互貿易關係的一種書面協議。

market economy　市場經濟

市場經濟（又稱為自由市場經濟或自由企業經濟）是一種經濟體系，在這種體系下產品和服務的生產及銷售完全由自由市場的自由價格機制所引導，而不是像計劃經濟一般由國家所引導。市場經濟也被當作資本主義的同義詞。

4. Famous Quotes 名人語錄

We must ensure that the global market is embedded in broadly shared values and practices that reflect global social needs, and that all the world's people share the benefits of globalization.

Kofi Annan

我們必須確保內含全球市場的通用價值與做法要能反映出全世界的社會需求，還有所有世人要皆能共享全球化的利益。

科菲‧安南

It has been said that arguing against globalization is like arguing against the laws of gravity.

Kofi Annan

有人說反對全球化的言論就像是反對有地心引力的辯論一樣。

科菲・安南

. . . .

In too many instances, the march to globalization has also meant the marginalization of women and girls. And that must change.

Hillary Clinton

太多例子顯示出，全面進行全球化也意味了婦女與女孩的邊緣化，這是需要改變的一點。

希拉蕊・科林頓

. . . .

If you're totally illiterate and living on one dollar a day, the benefits of globalization never come to you.

Jimmy Carter

如果你完全看不懂字，每天只能靠一塊美元過活，你是絕對不會得到任何全球化的好處的。

吉米・卡特

Unit 3　Automation
自動化

1. Dialogue 實境對話　1-3

A: Yesterday in the "Computex Taipei" I saw a robot that can practice English with a beginner student.

B: You mean that the robot can talk with the English learner and correct mistakes?

A: Yes. In the demonstration I saw, the machine could interact with the students and remember their language patterns as well.

B: How smart! Do you think that robots will take the place of human English teachers soon?

A: The robot is still in the early phase of researching and developing. Right now, the machine can only work as an assistant, not as an instructor by itself.

B: Would you want to practice English with a robot?

A: I wouldn't, but I understand that sometimes, in some places, it is difficult to find a real person to practice English conversation with.

B: A real human English instructor is irreplaceable to me as well.

A: But the English-teaching robot has some good points, too. For example, the machine seldom makes grammatical mistakes and is always very patient in repeating exercises.

B: What else can the teaching robot do better than a human English teacher?

A: They say the language teaching robot can record the patterns of the students' mistakes and test them afterwards.

B: It sounds like the robot can make a good tutor.

中文翻譯

A： 昨天我在台北國際電腦展看見一個可以和初學者練習英語的機器人。

B： 你的意思是說這個機器人可以和英語學習者對話，而且糾正錯誤？

A： 沒錯，我看見機器人示範與學生互動的過程，而且還能夠記住學習者的語言模式。

B： 你聰明！你認為機器人很快就會取代真人英語老師嗎？

A： 這個機器人還在早期的研發階段，現在這機器人只能當助教，還不能單獨擔任教師。

B： 你會想要和機器人練習英語嗎？

A： 我不會，但是我知道在有些地方，有時候，很難找到一個真人來練習英語會話。

B： 對我而言，真人英語教師也是無法取代的。

A：但是機器人英語教師也有些優點，例如，機器人很少會犯文法錯誤，而且總能很有耐心地重覆練習。

B：機器人英語教師還有什麼比真人英語老師還要好的地方嗎？

A：聽說語言教學機器人能夠記錄學生的犯錯模式，然後測試學生。

B：聽起來這機器人很適合當個稱職的家教。

字彙與片語

- exhibition [ˌɛksə'bɪʃən] n. 展覽；展示會
- robot ['robət] n. 機器人
- demonstration [ˌdɛmən'streʃən] n. 實地示範
- instructor [ɪn'strʌktɚ] n. 教師；指導者
- irreplaceable [ˌɪrɪ'plesəb!] a. 不能替代的

2.Article 文章

Automation

Ever since the arrival of computer technology, automation has been a popular topic in all industries. Factory workers are threatened by programed robotics that might replace them; professionals are afraid of being made redundant by specific software of their trades, such as accounting and photography.

Automation has the characteristics of efficiency and precision that the blue-collar workers and office workers in the past might not have. Some say that computer technology will progress at such a fast pace that many professionals will lose their jobs soon. However, that has not been the case. For example, many doctors now can treat patients more efficiently with specialized computer systems. Quite a few consumers still prefer to buy hand-made watches and shoes, in spite of those items' relatively high prices. To them, such items made with craftsmanship have much better quality than digitally made products. Artificial intelligence has not stolen jobs from those with traditional professions as some fear; on the contrary, it has assisted and enhanced many practitioners in those fields.

It is true that computers and machines have become smarter than ever, but at the moment we see no signs that they will completely replace humans in the job market in the near future. At the rate of technological advances, it is very likely that people are capable of working side by side with computers and robots, as they have been for a long time.

自動化

自從電腦科技來臨，自動化一直是所有產業的熱門話題。工廠勞工受到程式設計好的機器人可能取而代之的威脅；專業人士擔心會因為其產業的特定軟體而被迫失業，例如會計與攝影。

自動化之高效率與精準的特徵，可能是從前的藍領勞工與辦公室員工所欠缺的。有人認為，電腦科技會進展如此快速，以致於很多專業人士將很快面臨失業，但是並非完全如此。例如，現在很多醫師可以使用專業的電腦系統使看診更有效率；不少消費者仍然偏愛手工製的手錶與鞋子，即使這些物件的價錢相對來說較高，對他們來說，這些師傅所做的精品比數位化產品的品質好得太多了。人工智慧並沒有偷走傳統產業工作者的職位，如同有些人擔心的那般，相反地，人工智慧對從事這些領域的人有很大的幫忙與助益。

電腦與機器已經變得比從前聰明得多，這點是正確的，但是照目前看來，我們在短期內看不到人類在就業市場上會完全被取代的徵兆，按照科技進步的速度看來，人類非常可能有能力與電腦與機器人共同合作，就如同由來已久那般。

- automation [ˌɔtə'meʃən] n. 自動化
- redundant [rɪ'dʌndənt] a. 多餘的；（因人員過剩而）被解僱的
- magnify ['mægnəˌfaɪ] v. 放大，擴大
- enhance [ɪn'hæns] v. 提高，增加

3. Terminology 財經專業術語

robotics　機器人學

機器人學是與機器人設計、製造、應用相關的科學，又稱爲機器人技術或機器人工程學，主要研究機器人的控制與其運用。

industrial engineering (IE)　工業工程

工業工程是研究由人、物料、資訊、設備、能源構成的合成系統，應用到數學、物理學、社會科學等的知識和技能，結合工程分析和設計的原理與方法，來預測與衡量這一合成系統能得到的結果。

production system　生產系統

所謂生產系統，是指在正常情況下支持日常業務運作的資訊系統，包括生產數據、數據處理系統、生產網路等等。一個企業的生產系統一般都具有創新、承續性、自我改良、環境保護等功能，生產系統在運作一段時間後需要改良，改良範圍一般包括改進產品的品質、加工方法、操作方法、生產方式等等。

🥤conveyor belt　傳送帶

17 世紀中，美國開始應用架空索道來輸送散狀物料，此後，傳送帶輸送機受到機械製造、電機、化工、冶金工業技術進步的影響，不斷改進，發展到在企業內部、企業之間，甚至城市之間的物料搬運，現為物料搬運系統機械化和自動化不可缺少的組成部分。

4. Famous Quotes 名人語錄

The first rule of any technology used in a business is that automation applied to an efficient operation will magnify the efficiency. The second is that automation applied to an inefficient operation will magnify the inefficiency.

Bill Gates

在商業上運用科技的第一原則是：自動化用於有效率的運作可以增加效率，第二原則：自動化用於缺乏效率的運作只會使其更缺乏效率。

比爾・蓋茲

For the blue-collar worker, the driving force behind change was factory automation using programmable machine tools. For the office worker, it's office automation using computer technology: enterprise-resource-planning systems, groupware, intranets, extranets; expert systems, the Web, and e-commerce.

Tom Peters

　　對於藍領階級來說，驅動改變的是工廠自動化，它運用了設定好程式的機器工具；對於辦公室員工來說，辦公室自動化是使用電腦科技：企業資源規劃系統、團隊軟體、企業內部網、外聯網、專家系統、網際網路、電子商務。

湯姆・彼得斯

．．

In many cases, jobs that used to be done by people are going to be able to be done through automation. I don't have an answer to that. That's one of the more perplexing problems of society.

John Sculley

　　很多從前靠人做的工作將會為機器自動化生產而取代，對此我沒有任何解答，這是一個較複雜的社會問題。

湯姆・斯卡利

．．

All in all, I don't think robots and greater automation can bring about a utopian world as I imagined it would as a kid 50 years ago.

Stanley Druckenmiller

　　總而言之，我不像五十年前還是小孩時那樣，認為機器人和更多的自動化會帶來烏托邦社會。

史坦力・杜魯肯米勒

Unit 4　The Drop in Oil Prices
油價下跌

1. Dialogue 實境對話

 1-4

A: Have you noticed that the drop in oil prices has been in the news a lot recently?

B: Yes, but I don't see how lower oil prices affect our daily lives.

A: You might think the oil issue does not relate to you, but quite a few industries have already profited from the plunge of oil prices.

B: Really? Can you give me some examples?

A: Airlines, shipping companies and other transportation companies have directly benefited from falling oil prices.

B: But I haven't noticed any remarkably lower airfares among the airlines.

A: That's because the market is dominated by a few major airline companies. How about in the retail and hospitality industries? Surely you have seen more travelers around, who spend more money than before.

B: Consumers go out in general more than before, but I am not so sure if that comes from the drop in oil prices.

A: It's indirectly related to falling oil prices. Plus, there is one industry that is most likely to experience a boost because of lower oil prices: the auto industry.

B: Maybe you are right. Two of my neighbors bought new cars recently, and quite high-end ones.

A: Auto makers are able to sell cars much more easily when oil prices are low, including trucks.

B: I see your point.

A: Besides, the lower the shipping costs, the more attractive the prices of products become.

B: As it has turned out, for the energy industry the drop in oil prices is not such a good thing, but for other industries, the effects might be positive.

中文翻譯

A： 你是否注意到最近新聞常報導油價下跌？

B： 我注意到了，但是我還是不明白油價下跌與我們日常生活之間的關係。

A： 你可能以為油價問題與你無關，但是相當多的產業都已經因油價降低而獲利。

B： 真的嗎？你可以為我舉些例子嗎？

A： 航空公司、貨運公司跟其它運輸公司都已直接因油價下跌獲利。

B： 但是我沒有注意到航空公司的機票有任何明顯的下降。

A： 那是因為市場為幾家主要航空公司主導的緣故，那麼零售業與服務業呢？你一定注意到周圍的觀光客變多了，他們的消費能力也變強了。

B： 比起之前，整體來說消費者更常外出，但是我不是很確定那是因為油價下跌的緣故。

A： 這與油價下滑間接有關係。還有一項產業最可能因為油價下跌而成長：汽車製造業。

B： 或許你說的對，最近我有兩個鄰居都買了新車，而且是相當高檔的車。

A： 油價低時，汽車製造業比較能夠賣出車子，包含卡車在內。

B： 我明白你的意思。

A： 除此之外，運費越低，產品價格就變得越吸引人。

B： 結果，對能源產業來說，油價下跌並非是件好事，但是對其它產業來說，影響可能是正面的。

- relate [rɪ'let] v. 有關，涉及
- remarkable [rɪ'mɑrkəb!] a. 值得注意的
- dominate ['dɑmə,net] v. 支配，控制
- boost [bust] v. 提高；增加
- turn out 結果成為

2. Article 文章

Industries that Profit from Lower Oil Prices

Certain industries have profited from the drop in oil prices. This includes those industries which directly gain more revenues from the lower costs of oil, such as airlines and transportation. Other industries gain higher profitability because consumers can use the money saved from oil-related purchases to spend on their products or services. The following are five of the main industries which profit from low oil prices.

Airlines: The lower costs of jet fuel contribute to the higher profits of most airline companies. Due to the dominance of major airline companies in the market, airfares have not dropped, but the airline companies are making huge profits. This is reflected in the increase of airline stock prices.

Transportation: Shipping companies, freight trucks and marine companies all save costs because of lower oil prices. Many companies that rely on shipping services gain direct margins from less spending on oil.

Retail: As customers save money on many oil products, they can spend more money on food and drinks in the retail industry. This can lift the domestic economy as a whole and can contribute to the stability of society.

Leisure: When basic staples are covered, customers have more disposable income at hand. They are more likely to spend money on entertainment, restaurants, travel, and the hospitality industry. When people travel abroad, they give an economic stimulus to the destination countries.

Auto: Auto makers are able to sell cars much more easily when oil costs are low. Lower oil prices make larger and more expensive vehicles more attractive than the smaller and fuel-efficient models. So far, the sales performances of most auto companies have hit record highs.

As seen above, the drop in oil prices has contributed to the economic boost in many industries directly or indirectly impacted by crude oil.

因油價下跌而獲利的產業

　　某些產業已經因為油價下跌而獲利，這些包括直接因為油價降低而增加營收的產業，例如航空業者與運輸業；還有一些產業，因為消費者在石油相關產品的支出減少，因而可以將省下的錢用來購買其產品或服務。以下為五種因為低油價而獲利的重要產業：

　　航空業者：飛機燃料的費用下降使得航空公司的利潤提高，因為主要航空公司的主導市場，機票費用尚未下降，但是航空公司獲利甚高，這一點可以由航空公司股票價格上升反映出來。

　　運輸業：貨運公司、貨運卡車、海運公司都因油價下跌而節省成本，很多倚賴貨運服務的公司都因為油價支出減少而直接獲利。

　　零售業：消費者可以將於石油相關產品上所節省的錢，花在零售業的食物與飲料上，這樣可以提振國內整體的經濟，可以對社會穩定有所助益。

　　休閒娛樂業：消費者在滿足了基本生活需要後，手上有了多餘的錢做消費，可以將錢花在娛樂、餐飲、旅遊、服務業上；人們到國外旅行時，也刺激了目的地的經濟。

　　汽車製造業：油價比從前低時，汽車製造業可以賣出更多的車；油價降低使得較大、較貴的汽車比小型省電的車種更吸引人，至今大部分汽車製造業者的業績已經創史上新高。

由以上可知，無論直接或間接受到原油影響的產業，很多產業都因油價下跌而得以提升獲利。

字彙與片語

- revenue ['rɛvəˌnju] n. 收入，收益
- marine [mə'rin] a. 海運的
- stability [stə'bɪlətɪ] n. 穩定，穩定性
- stimulus ['stɪmjələs] n. 刺激
- contribute [kən'trɪbjut] v. 貢獻，出力

3. Terminology 財經專業術語

OPEC　石油輸出國組織

石油輸出國組織是一個自願結成的政府間組織，對其成員國的石油政策進行協調、統一。1960 年 9 月，伊朗、伊拉克、科威特、沙特阿拉伯、委內瑞拉的代表在巴格達開會，決定聯合起來共同對付西方石油公司，以及反對國際石油壟斷資本的控制與剝削，以維護石油收入。14 日，五國宣告成立石油輸出國組織，總部設在維也納。1962 年 11 月 6 日，石油輸出國組織在聯合國秘書處備案，成為正式的國際組織，同時，隨著成員的增加，石油輸出國組織發展成為亞洲、非洲、拉丁美洲一些主要石油生產國的國際性石油組織。石油輸

出國組織的宗旨：協調和統一各成員國的石油政策，並確定以最適宜的手段來維護成員國各自與共同的利益。

supply and demand　供給和需求

供給和需求是一個經濟學模型，用來作為決定市場均衡價格和均衡產量。這個模型適用於競爭性市場，而不適用於市場存在壟斷或寡頭壟斷的情況，需求或供給價格分別由消費者的需求量和生產者的供給量所決定，形成市場兩種力量決定價格和產量的均衡。

energy crisis　能源危機

能源危機是指因為能源供應短缺或是價格上漲而影響經濟，通常涉及到石油、電力或其他自然資源的短缺。能源危機通常會使得經濟震盪，很多突如其來的經濟衰退通常就是由能源危機引起的，事實上，電力的生產價格的上漲導致生產成本的增加；汽車或其他交通工具所使用的石油產品價格的上漲，則會降低了消費者的消費意願。

energy conservation　節約能源

節約能源（簡稱節能）是指以減少能源消耗的方式，保護資源，減少對環境的污染。透過提高能源使用效率，減少能源消耗，或降低傳統能源的消耗量可以達到節約能源的目的。

4. Famous Quotes 名人語錄

Oil prices have certainly become a threat for the world economy.

Rodrigo Rato

油價顯然成為世界經濟的一大威脅。

羅多格 · 拉圖

We will work to bring an element of stability to the price of oil.

Olusegun Obasanjo

我們該努力讓油價穩定下來。

歐陸塞根 · 歐巴山久

Over time, there's a very close correlation between what happens to the dollar and what happens to the price of oil. When the dollar gets weak, the price of oil, which, as you know, and other commodities are denominated in dollars, they go up. We saw it in the '70s, when the dollar was savagely weakened.

Steve Forbes

長久下來，美元的變化與油價有著極為密切關係，眾所周知，當美元下跌時，油價與以美元定價的原物料價格會上漲，這在 1970 年代美元嚴重下跌時就發生過。

史蒂夫 · 富比世

The one thing people seem to forget is the more oil we have, the lower the price and the lower the profits the oil companies make.

David Pratt

人們似乎忘了，我們擁有的石油越多，油價與石油公司的獲利也就越低。

大衛 · 帕拉德

Unit 5 Deepening Income Inequality
收入不平等日益嚴重

1. Dialogue 實境對話
 1-5

A: If I had a salary like yours, I'd be really happy.

B: Do you know how many hours a week I have to work for that pay?

A: Your work seems very flexible, and as a salesperson you can meet clients often in a café or in a restaurant.

B: That's hard work, you know.

A: I wish I could make as much money as you do.

B: In the sales department, I am the person who makes the least money. My year-end bonus cannot compare with theirs.

A: Don't be so hard on yourself. You just began this work last year.

B: Thanks. It's like a rat race, especially as a salesperson in this industry.

A: Do you feel happier working in your current company compared to the last one?

B: Not really. My salary has increased, but I don't have time to enjoy it.

A: Maybe it is because you cannot stop comparing yourself to other salespeople in your department.

B: Maybe. What's worrying me is that I haven't spent enough time with my wife and two small kids.

A: Now you make me feel a little better about myself. I always finish my work on time and get to be with my family whenever I'm off work.

B: From that perspective, you can say that you are spiritually richer than me.

中文翻譯

A： 如果我的薪水有你的那麼高，我會非常高興。

B： 你知道我一星期要工作多少小時，才能有那樣的收入呢？

A： 你的工作似乎很有彈性，而且你是業務，通常可以和客戶在咖啡廳或餐廳碰面。

B： 不過這還是份辛苦的工作，這點你是知道的。

A： 真希望能有辦法賺跟你一樣多的錢。

B： 在業務部門，我賺的錢最少，我的年終獎金無法與其他業務的相比。

A： 不要對自己要求過高，你從去年才剛開始這份工作。

B： 謝謝，這真是永無止盡的競賽，特別是對這行的業務來說。

A： 你覺得在目前這家公司工作比在上一家公司快樂嗎？

B： 並沒有，我的薪水是增加了，但是我沒有時間來享用這些錢。

A： 或許這是因為你無法停止與部門的其他業務比較吧。

B： 或許吧。讓我煩心的是，沒有花足夠時間來和妻子與兩個小小孩
　　相處。

A： 這樣讓我對自己感到好過些了，我總是準時下班，工作時間外我
　　都能隨時和我家人在一起。

B： 從那個角度看來，你大可以說，你在精神上比我富足。

字彙與片語

- inequality [ˌɪnɪˈkwɑlətɪ] n. 不均等；不平等
- flexible [ˈflɛksəb!] a. 有彈性的
- year-end bonus 年終獎金
- perspective [pɚˈspɛktɪv] n. 看法，觀點
- spiritually [ˈspɪrɪtʃʊəlɪ] adv. 精神上

Deepening Income Inequality

The gap between the rich and the poor has grown wider than ever. In America, the wealthiest 1% of the population owns most of the country's fortune. In such an economically unequal and divided society, most people, particularly those at the bottom, become more and more dissatisfied.

Some people believe that deepening income inequality is one of the problems a country's government must address. Nevertheless, businesses can improve the situation significantly by abiding by the minimum wages, hiring more women and minorities, and providing adequate employee benefits. Corporations that deal with income inequality in the ways mentioned above create more opportunities for their staff and for themselves. Overall, from a business perspective, providing employees with equitable benefits will promote a healthy corporate culture, which increases productivity and profits in return.

Unequal distribution of wealth has divided society into different classes with unjust and unequal access to resources, such as education and healthcare. The government cannot solve this worsening social issue on its own, and business owners can no longer ignore their responsibilities in this area.

收入不平等日益嚴重

收入不平等的問題越來越嚴重，全美國 1% 最富有的人擁有整個國家最多的資產。在這樣經濟不平等且分裂的社會裡，大部分人，特別是在社會最低下階層的人，變得越來越不滿。

有些人認為收入日益不平等是政府的問題，然而，企業界能藉著遵守最低薪資、多雇用婦女與少數族群、提供充足的員工福利，來大幅改善這個問題。用上述方式處理收入不均問題的企業能為其員工和公司創造更多的機會，整體而言，從企業角度來說，提供員工平等福利的公司會促進健康的企業文化，最終提高生產力與利潤。

財富不平等的分配使得社會分裂為不同的階級，能夠獲得的資源不公平且不平等，例如教育與健康保險的資源。政府無法獨自解決這個日益嚴重的社會問題，而企業家不能再忽視這方面的責任。

字彙與片語

- gap [gæp] n. 差距
- abide by 遵從；遵守
- the minimum wage 最低工資
- distribution [ˌdɪstrəˈbjuʃən] n. 分配
- access [ˈæksɛs] n. 進入；進入的權利
- worsen [ˈwɝsn] v. 惡化

3. Terminology 財經專業術語

income inequality　收入不平等

亦稱為貧富懸殊、貧富不均、經濟不平等，是指一個群體裡每個人之間的財富及收入的分配不均等，一般是指一個社會裡個人或群體之間的收入差距，但亦可用來指國際貧富懸殊，此現象與經濟平等與公平機會的概念有關。

income distribution　收入分配

收入分配廣義上指在一定時期內經濟活動成果在各經濟主體之間的分配。

social inequality　社會不平等

指的是一個社會當中，某些群體的社會地位、社會階級、社交圈遭到限制或傷害，社會不平等涉及的範疇包括擁有私有產權、投票權、言論自由、集會自由，以及獲取教育、醫療、住處、交通、旅遊、假期等等的機會。

social mobility　社會流動

社會流動指個人在階層裡向上或向下的流動情形，通常是以經濟、聲望作為主要區隔的因素。社會學注重社會流動的重心為在一個社會當中流動的數量與頻率，這包含世代間流動頻率的不同，同時亦能檢視社會開放的程度。

 4. Famous Quotes 名人語錄

Income inequality is troubling because, among other things, it means that many people in our society don't have the opportunities to advance themselves.

Ben Bernanke

收入不平等令人不安，因為其所帶來最大的問題是，我們社會上有很多人無法獲得晉升的機會。

班・柏南克

The best solution to income inequality is providing a high-quality education for everybody. In our highly technological, globalized economy, people without education will not be able to improve their economic situation.

Ben Bernanke

最好解決收入不平等的辦法是提供所有人高品質的教育。我們處於高科技與全球化的經濟，缺乏教育的人將無法改善他們自身的經濟狀況。

班・柏南克

Increasing inequality in income distribution in this country has broader policy implications, and there is also the growing problem of perverse incentives that result from executives receiving grossly disproportionate compensation based on decisions they themselves take.

Barney Frank

我們這個國家收入分配不平等日益嚴重，這代表了更大的政策問題，還有一個日漸嚴重的不良動機，那就是主管階級可自行決定自己完全不成比例的高收入。

巴爾尼・法蘭克

· ·

The difference between rich and poor is becoming more extreme, and as income inequality widens the wealth gap in major nations, education, health and social mobility are all threatened.

Helene D. Gayle

貧富差距日益極端化，而且因為收入不平等會使得主要國家的貧富懸殊更惡化，使得教育、健康、社會流動性都受到威脅。

海倫・基・蓋爾

Chapter 2 Marketing
行銷

Unit 1 Basic Marketing 基本行銷

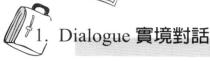

1. Dialogue 實境對話 2-1

A: How is your marketing plan for my Bed & Breakfast going?

B: Well, I think word of mouth is the most effective way to advertise.

A: This Bed & Breakfast is brand new and about to start in a week. How could we possibly have enough customer feedback within such a short period of time?

B: Maybe we could attract guests with little or no fees during the trial run.

A: Little or no fees!

B: That's right. The guests will have to write customer feedback, which will be put on our Facebook page.

A: Let's hope these authentic pieces of feedback can bring us publicity.

B: The guests will be asked to take photos of the Bed & Breakfast, and we'll have a photography competition in the end.

A: Free coupons will be awarded to the winners to stay in the Bed & Breakfast.

B: They can give the free coupons as gifts to their friends as well.

A: How are you going to attract these guests to come here?

B: Through the Internet, of course.

中文翻譯

A： 關於我那間民宿的行銷計劃你進行得怎麼樣了？

B： 我認為口碑是最有效的廣告。

A： 這間民宿是全新的，而且要在一個星期後開始營業，我們怎麼可能在這麼短的時間內有很多客人的意見？

B： 或許我們能夠在試營運的時候用低價或免費吸引客人來。

A： 低價或免費！

B： 是的。客人必須要寫顧客意見，供我們放在臉書上。

A： 希望這些真實的意見能為我們帶來知名度。

B： 我們會要求這些客人拍民宿的照片，最後我們會舉辦一場攝影比賽。

A： 得獎者能獲得這間民宿的免費住宿券。

B： 也可以將這些免費住宿券送給朋友。

A： 你要如何吸引這些客人來呢？

B： 當然是靠網路。

- effective [ɪˈfɛktɪv] a. 有效的
- trial [ˈtraɪəl] a. 試驗的
- authentic [ɔˈθɛntɪk] a. 可信的，真實的，可靠的
- award [əˈwɔrd] v. 授予，給予
- coupon [ˈkupɑn] n. 優惠券；減價優待券

2. Article 文章

The Big Data and Marketing

Have you wondered why you often receive e-mails about the latest items you are considering purchasing? Such as the new books you would like to get ahold of and the restaurant discounts you just need on special occasions? Since the arrival of the Big Data, customer behaviors are being analyzed carefully with or without their consent. The companies which use the data analyses might know your purchase habits better than your spouses or partners do.

What impacts has the Big Data had on marketing? Marketing strategies and budgets have become more precise, and the total marketing spend is more under control. Market segmentation can be analyzed very exactly. Salespeople can accurately target prospective customers, including old customers and new ones. The Big Data has made it much easier and more scientific to predict sales performance.

Large enterprises with advanced technologies have started to collect and study such data, and soon the medium and small businesses will follow suit. Without a doubt, predictive analytics of data has become the main driving force of marketing in our modern digital times.

本文翻譯

大數據與行銷

你是否曾想過為什麼你會在剛好想買什麼東西的時候，收到相關的電子郵件呢？像是你正考慮要買的新書，還有你在特別節慶正需要的折價券？自從大數據時代來臨，無論消費者同意或不同意，他們的消費行為都被仔細分析。使用數據分析的公司可能比你的配偶或伴侶還了解你的購物習慣。

大數據對行銷有什麼影響？行銷策略和預算變得更精準，行銷總支出更容易控制，市場區隔得以分析得非常精準，業務人員可以準確地針對未來的消費者做推銷，包含老客戶與新客戶。大數據使得預測業績變得更容易，更科學化。

具有先進科技的大型企業已經開始收集並研究這些數據，很快地中小企業會跟進。無疑地，數據的預測性系統分析在我們現代數位化時代會成為行銷的主要驅動力。

- data ['detə] n. 資料，數據（datum 的名詞複數）
- consent [kən'sɛnt] n. 同意，贊成，答應
- impact ['ɪmpækt] n. 衝擊，撞擊，碰撞
- precise [prɪ'saɪs] a. 精確的；準確的；確切的
- segmentation [ˌsɛgmən'teʃən] n. 分割；區隔
- prospective [prə'spɛktɪv] a. 預期的；即將發生的
- analytics [ˌæn!'ɪtɪks] n. 解析學；分析論

3. Terminology 財經專業術語

target segmentation　市場區隔

市場區隔是經濟學和市場學的一種概念，指將客戶按照一個或幾個特點分類，使每類具有相似的產品或服務需求，同一個劃分具有相同需求，對市場刺激做出相似回應且對市場干預有反應。

direct marketing　直接行銷

直接行銷是指直接接觸目標客戶來推廣產品或服務，而不透過第三方做廣告來宣傳，通常的方式為郵寄、電子郵件、面對面溝通等，這種直接的方式非常省錢且有效，特別適合中小型服務業企業。

niche market　利基市場

利基市場就是一塊較小的區隔（小社圈的顧客群），有利潤而又專門性的市場。利基戰略則是指企業根據自身所特有的資源優勢，通過專業化經營來佔領這些市場，從而獲取最大限度的收益所採取的競爭戰略。

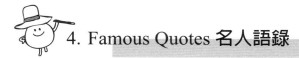

4. Famous Quotes 名人語錄

The aim of marketing is to know and understand the customer so well the product or service fits him and sells itself.

Peter Drucker

行銷的目的是為了完全瞭解客戶，使產品與服務因為符合客戶需求而自動銷售出去。

彼得・杜魯克

Word of mouth is the most valuable form of marketing, but you can't buy it. You can only deliver it. And you have to really deliver.

G-Eazy

口碑是最寶貴的行銷，但是你無法用錢買到，只能履行這個口碑，而且你必須真正去履行。

G-Eazy

Business has only two functions - marketing and innovation.

Milan Kundera

商業只有兩個功能：行銷和創新。

米蘭‧昆德拉

. . . .

And let's be clear: It's not enough just to limit ads for foods that aren't healthy. It's also going to be critical to increase marketing for foods that are healthy.

Michelle Obama

讓我們弄清楚這一點：光是限制不健康食品的廣告是不夠的；增加健康食品的行銷也是很重要的。

蜜雪兒‧歐巴馬

. . . .

Green issues have been used as a marketing tool. Sometimes these green claims are completely meaningless.

Frank Gehry

綠色議題曾被用來作爲行銷工具，有時候這些綠色主張根本完全沒有意義。

法蘭克‧蓋瑞

Unit 2 Brand Marketing
品牌行銷

1. Dialogue 實境對話 2-2

A: Why are you buying a sports shirt of this brand again? Don't you think it's way too expensive than other homemade brands?

B: I know, but its quality is also much better.

A: Are you sure? I think the only difference is the logo on the sports shirt.

B: The logo is also a sign of quality assurance, of course.

A: And a sign of conspicuous consumption.

B: A what?

A: A sign of conspicuous consumption. It means that you buy this item only to show off.

B: That's not true. I wear these sports shirts only when I am playing sports.

A: Then why are you such a loyal customer of this brand?

B: I wouldn't call myself loyal because I also buy clothes of other brands.

A: Other expensive Japanese brands as well.

B: Those clothes are all designed very well and made of good materials.

A: To me, they are quite similar to those I bought in the marketplace.

B: That's because you don't know how to appreciate fine clothing products.

A: You are right. I really cannot tell the differences.

中文翻譯

A： 你為什麼又買這個牌子的運動衫呢？你不會覺得比其他國產的牌子貴太多了嗎？

B： 我知道，但是品質也比較好。

A： 你確定嗎？我認為唯一不同點是運動衫上的商標。

B： 當然這個商標也是品質保證的標記。

A： 也是炫耀性消費的標記。

B： 你說什麼？

A： 炫耀性消費的標記，表示你買這個東西只是來擺闊。

B： 才不是，我只有在運動時才穿這些運動衫。

A： 那麼你為何要當這個品牌的忠實顧客呢？

B： 我不認為我是個忠實顧客，因為我也買其它牌子的衣服。

A： 其它昂貴的日本名牌。

B： 那些衣服都設計得很精美，料子都很好。

A： 對我來說，倒是跟我在市場上買的很相似。

B： 那是因為你不知道如何欣賞精緻的衣物。

A： 你說的對，我真的無法分辨其中的不同之處。

- homemade ['hom'med] a. 自製的；家裡做的；國產的
- logo ['logo] n. 商標，標誌
- assurance [ə'ʃʊrəns] n. 保證
- conspicuous [kən'spɪkjʊəs] a. 明顯的，易看見的；顯著的
- consumption [kən'sʌmpʃən] n. 消費

Building a Brand

Quite a few business owners talk about building a brand, but it seems that they don't really know what a brand stands for. To put it simply, a brand is the identity of the business and its values. All people who run businesses should think from time to time about how they want to define their businesses.

Branding is essential to all businesses. A strategically defined brand can easily attract customers who share the same or similar values, and they can therefore become loyal customers. Brands that are well-positioned toward the target customers are usually profitable. Such brand segmentation leads to higher sales performance.

A brand needs to be built and also, equally important, maintained, and this requires constantly monitoring customer satisfaction. When a brand is gradually losing its original identity, customers can feel it right away. In the age of social media, building a brand has often been a process with the heavy involvement of customers.

本文翻譯

品牌的建立

許多企業的業主都在討論建立品牌，但是很多人都似乎不明白品牌的意義，簡單來說，品牌為企業與其價值的身分。所有經營企業的人都該想想要如何定義其企業。

　　品牌的建立對所有企業來說都極為重要，一個在策略上界定清楚的品牌可以輕易吸引對其價值認同的客戶，這些客戶能因此成為忠實客戶。能針對客戶設計的品牌通常能獲利，這樣的品牌區隔帶來高銷售業績。

　　品牌需要建立，同樣重要的，也需要去維護，必須不斷檢視客戶滿意度。當品牌漸漸失去原有的特色，顧客可以馬上感覺到，在這個社群網站的時代，建立品牌通常需要顧客的大量參與。

字彙與片語

- identity [aɪ'dɛntətɪ] n. 身分；個性，特性
- profitable ['prɑfɪtəb!] a. 有利的，贏利的
- maintain [men'ten] v. 維持；保持
- original [ə'rɪdʒən!] a. 最初的，本來的；原始的
- involvement [ɪn'vɑlvmənt] n. 參與

3. Terminology 財經專業術語

brand　品牌

　　傳統的觀點是根據行銷大師菲立普・柯特勒（Philip Kotler）的經典之作《行銷管理》（Marketing Management）而來的。柯特勒

在書中寫道：「品牌代表著一個名字、名詞、符號、象徵、設計，甚或是這些東西的總和，企業希望藉著品牌能夠讓別人辨別出產品或服務所歸屬的公司，並且和競爭者的產品有所區隔。」

 brand marketing　品牌行銷

　　品牌行銷是通過市場行銷，使客戶對企業品牌和產品或服務獲得了解，進而願意花錢購買，企業也就能得到讓產品或服務有實踐諾言的機會。

4. Famous Quotes 名人語錄

For a truly effective social campaign, a brand needs to embrace the first principles of marketing, which involves brand definition and consistent storytelling.

Simon Mainwaring

　　為了要使社會宣傳活動真正有效，一個品牌必須要擁抱行銷的最基本原則，這牽涉到對品牌的定義和不斷講述故事。

賽門・媚瓦林

I don't think of myself as a brand. Branding to me feels like a position or identity that's frozen in time. I'm more interested in transitions.

David Rockwell

我不認為自己是個品牌，品牌對我來說像是個在歲月中凍結的立場或身分認同，而我對於轉變比較感興趣。

大衛・洛克衛爾

....

The response to the Starbucks brand has been phenomenal in our international markets.

Howard Schultz

我們的國際市場對於星巴克這個品牌的反應非常驚人。

霍華・舒茲

....

Our history is based on extending the brand to categories within the guardrails of Starbucks.

Howard Schultz

我們有史以來一直不斷在星巴克的範圍內擴展這個品牌。

霍華・舒茲

....

Journalists seem mostly interested in what brand of shoes I wear.

Rem Koolhaas

記者似乎對我所穿的鞋子是什麼品牌最感興趣。

雷姆・庫哈斯

Unit 3 Creative Marketing
創意行銷

 1. Dialogue 實境對話 2-3

A: Have any of you come up with an idea for marketing the facial cream?

B: The facial cream from Australia is designed for mature female customers. I suggest, in the beginning, we give away some samples to mature female buyers, who purchase other products from us.

A: In that case, the customers who haven't heard of our brand will never have the chance to try out the facial cream.

B: Of course, it is not enough to give free samples; at the same time, we should put up advertisements to promote this product.

A: Since the facial cream is designed for women above age 50, we should use traditional media to attract customers, such as TV commercials, newspaper or magazines.

B: Not to forget that many of the potential buyers do surf online and even enjoy mobile shopping.

A: Do you have any other creative ideas to market this facial cream?

B: The best way I can think of is to package the facial cream together with our other hot items.

A: That's a good idea. If we'd create a gift set, what would you suggest me to put in with it?

B: Maybe a quality hand cream and a body lotion.

A: What makes the set stand out?

B: The facial cream features pure herbs from Australia. The set could be called "Natural Feel from Down Under."

A: That sounds terrific. Mother's Day is coming up, and we should capitalize on the occasion.

B: In that case, I'll use our Facebook page and launch the sales campaign as soon as possible!

中文翻譯

A： 你想出了這款面霜的行銷點子了嗎？

B： 這款來自澳大利亞的面霜是針對熟齡女性所設計的，我建議在剛開始時送些樣品給買我們其它產品的熟女顧客。

A： 那樣的話，沒有聽過我們牌子就沒有機會試用我們的面霜。

B： 當然，只送免費樣品是不夠的，同時我們應該登廣告來宣傳這個產品。

A： 既然這款面霜是針對五十歲以上女性所設計的，我們就應該使用傳統的媒體來吸引顧客，例如電視廣告、報紙、雜誌。

B： 不要忘了很多潛在客戶還是會上網，甚至喜愛用手機購物。

A： 你是否有其它行銷這款面霜的創意？

B： 我能想到最後的方式就是將這款面霜跟其它熱賣商品包裝在一起推出。

A： 真是個好主意。如果我們要組裝成禮物盒，你會建議我放什麼進去呢？

B： 高品質的護手霜和身體乳液或許不錯。

A： 這樣的禮盒有什麼特色？

B： 這款面霜以澳大利亞的草藥為特色，這禮盒可以稱為「澳洲天然風」。

A： 聽起來真不錯。母親節快到了，我們應該要好好利用這個節日。

B： 那麼讓我盡快用臉書來推出這場特賣活動。

字彙與片語

- commercial [kə'mɝʃəl] n. 商業廣告
- potential [pə'tɛnʃəl] a. 潛在的，可能的
- feature [fitʃɚ] v. 以……為特色
- capitalize ['kæpət!ˌaɪz] v. 利用
- launch [lɔntʃ] v. 開始；積極投入

Creative Marketing

In creative marketing, the objectives are to provide the target audience with pleasantly surprising effects. Take the example of small surprise gifts. If someone receives a poster of movie stars upon buying a ticket to a movie, that would delight most movie-goers. Sometimes, a surprising, thoughtful service works better than any complimentary gift.

The strategies of creative marketing can be as numerous as one imagines, and they center on how to best deliver the advertising messages creatively. Here are two good examples: in a boutique, some designer dresses and bags are labeled as limited editions to emphasize the scarcity of the items; also, it is not uncommon to see young models with little clothing or outrageous outfits walking on a street for an advertising campaign. Whether it works or not is totally up to customers' responses.

Timing plays an important role in any creative marketing campaign. Sales seasons like Christmas and Lunar New Year are two of the biggest buying cycles in a year. Creative marketing strategies work best with the right timing. If the creativity put into marketing strategies does not generate sales revenues eventually, the time and effort is all in vain.

創意行銷

創意行銷時之目的就是要讓鎖定的觀眾感到驚喜，就拿驚奇小禮物的例子來說，如果在買電影票時收到電影明星的海報，就會讓大部分人感到很高興；有時候，出乎意料之外的貼心服務產生之效果比任何免費禮物還要好。

創意行銷的策略可以多到數不清，重點是如何以最有創意的方式來傳達訊息。以下為兩個很好的例子：在精品店，有些設計師設計的洋裝和提包會標明限量款來強調數量有限；還有，經常可以看見年輕模特兒穿著清涼，甚至誇張的衣物，走在街上來宣傳特賣活動。至於廣告效果成功與否，則有待消費者的反應來決定。

除此之外，時間控制在創意行銷活動中扮演非常重要的角色，像是聖誕節和農曆新年就是兩個重大的特賣週期，創意行銷要配合良好的時機才能有最佳效果。如果行銷策略中的創意最終無法使業績成長，那麼投入的心力與時間也都是徒勞無功。

- complimentary [ˌkɑmpləˈmɛntərɪ] a. 贈送的，免費的
- numerous [ˈnjumərəs] a. 許多的，很多的
- campaign [kæmˈpen] n. 活動
- outrageous [aʊtˈredʒəs] a. 令人吃驚的
- cycle [ˈsaɪk!] n. 週期；循環

3. Terminology 財經專業術語

creativity 創意

創意指對創業的一種新想法或新點子，並據此所做的進一步構想或方案。創意是創業設計誕生的開始，因此，創業設計者應從各個方面廣泛收集各種創意，以免埋沒或遺漏好的商機。

media creativity 媒體創意

媒體創意是指為大眾傳播媒體以及媒體經營與管理提供創新性策略和構想，媒體創意包括了媒體的製作、傳播、經營管理的創意，應用於整個傳播媒體領域裡。

the cultural and creative industries 文化創意產業

簡稱「文創產業」，顧名思義，為結合了文化及創意的產業，「文化」一詞有諸多不同的定義，廣義來說，泛指在一個社會中共同生活

的人們，擁有相近的生活習慣、風俗民情，以及信仰等；狹義的來說，即是指「藝術」，是一種經由人們創造出來新型態的產物。不論就狹義或廣義的文化而言，「文化創意」即是指在既有存在的文化中，加入每個國家、族群、個人等創意，賦予文化新的風貌與價值。

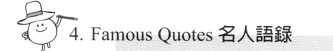 experiential marketing　經驗行銷

經驗行銷是從消費者的感官、情感、思考、行動、聯想五個方面重新定義，設計營銷理念，讓消費者參與品牌發展和行銷過程，目的是要讓他們與品牌產生緊密的聯結。消費者消費時是理性和感性兼具的，消費者在消費前、消費中、消費後的體驗是研究消費者行為與企業品牌經營的關鍵。

4. Famous Quotes 名人語錄

The best way to predict the future is to create it.

Peter Drucker

預言未來的最佳方法就是去創造未來。

彼得・杜魯克

An essential aspect of creativity is not being afraid to fail.

Edwin Land

發揮創意最重要的就是不要怕失敗。

愛德衛 · 蘭德

....

Good marketing makes the company look smart. Great marketing makes the customer feel smart.

Joe Chernov

好的行銷讓企業顯得聰明；絕佳的行銷讓消費者感到自己很聰明。

喬 · 徹爾諾夫

....

The best marketing doesn't feel like marketing.

Tom Fishburne

最好的行銷讓人覺得不像是行銷。

湯姆 · 費雪柏爾恩

....

Make your marketing so useful people would pay you for it.

Jay Baer

使你的行銷有效到讓人願意付費。

傑 · 拜爾

1. Dialogue 實境對話

2-4

A: Kevin, some of your colleagues raised the issue of your pictures on Facebook.

B: I know, some pictures were taken when I was working as a model for a men's underwear company. At that time, I was desperately short of cash.

A: Why did you put them on your personal Facebook page then?

B: My manager at the time suggested it, in order to attract more customers.

A: Now you are the new spokesperson for a multinational company. How would your audience think of you after seeing photos with you in underwear?

B: I am terribly sorry, but at that time, I really didn't think it would become such a serious problem.

A: Not to mention your colleagues who have been talking about this behind your back for quite a while.

B: What should I do now? I need this job, and I'm sure I'm competent for it.

A: Remove the near-naked pictures immediately! I'll arrange a small press conference for you to explain this issue sincerely.

B: Thank you very much. I'll do it.

A: This is a lesson for you to learn more about media management. As a spokesperson, you have to be more careful than others about what to do and what not to do.

B: That's right. The pictures were posted years ago, and I thought nobody would notice them anyway.

A: Be smart when you deal with social media next time!

中文翻譯

A：凱文，有些同事對你臉書上的照片有意見。

B：我知道，有些照片是我當男性內褲公司模特兒所拍的照片，在那個時候我非常缺錢。

A：那你為什麼要放在臉書上呢？

B：那時候的經理建議我這麼做，好吸引顧客。

A：現在你身為跨國公司的新發言人，你的聽眾要是看到你穿內褲的照片後，會怎麼想你呢？

B：真抱歉，但是那個時候我真的沒有想到會變成這麼嚴重的問題。

A：更不用提你的同事，他們已經在你背後談這個問題很久了。

B：現在我該怎麼辦？我需要這份工作，而且我確定我有能力做好。

A：馬上將這些照片撤下！我會安排一場小型記者會，讓你誠心地解釋這件事。

B：非常感謝，我會照著做。

A： 這是你關於媒體管理學到的一個教訓，身為發言人，你要比別人更明白什麼是該做的，什麼是不該做的。

B： 你說的對，那些照片是幾年前發布上去的，我以為根本不會有人注意到。

A： 下次使用社群媒體時要放聰明點！

字彙與片語

- desperately [ˈdɛspərɪtlɪ] adv. 絕望地；不顧一切地，拼命地
- spokesperson [ˈspoksˌpɝsn] n. 發言人
- multinational [ˈmʌltɪˈnæʃən!] a. 多國的；跨國公司的
- competent [ˈkɑmpətənt] a. 能勝任的，稱職的
- press conference 記者會

How to Manage a Social Media Crisis

We live in an ever changing world, and it seems that almost all businesses experience one crisis or another at a certain point of time. With social media, all customers seem to be armed with the keyboard to make their voices heard. Have you thought about what to do if a social media crisis occurs unexpectedly? The following suggestions would be very practical to keep in mind.

First, make sure you have all staff respond to the complaining customers in a polite and diplomatic way. Of course, speed is essential. Quickly acknowledging that something went wrong can calm the anger of the frustrated customers. It is very important that you provide one channel, such as Facebook, to manage all the information coming in and out. Afterwards, the company can announce the methods of damage control on the same social media, with a short video recording of the president offering an apology put online if necessary. Be specific about the information you post online to tell customers how to have their purchased products exchanged or compensated.

They key point is to keep all employees informed about the crisis so that they know how to respond to the issue appropriately. Customers will generally accept the apology if they feel the company is sincerely sorry. All people in the company, including executives and employees, must learn lessons from the crisis. Customers might forgive you once, but probably not the second time.

本文翻譯

如何管理社群媒體危機

我們所處的世界瞬息萬變，幾乎所有企業都可能有時會遭遇危機，幾乎所有的消費者在鍵盤前都有在社群網站上發聲的武器，你是否想過，要是在社群媒體上忽然發生了危機該怎麼辦呢？以下幾個實用的建議可以牢記於心。

首先，要求所有員工對抱怨的客戶都要有禮貌且有技巧地回覆，時效當然非常重要，快速承認錯誤能使焦躁的顧客平靜下來。提供一個像臉書那樣的管道來管理進出的訊息是很重要的，然後，公司要能在同一社群媒體上宣布理賠的方式，如果必要的話，在網路上登出總裁道歉的錄影，而關於消費者已購買的產品要如何換貨或賠償的訊息要非常詳細。

最關鍵的一點就是要讓所有員工都知道這個危機，這樣他們才知道要如何妥善回應，如果顧客感受到企業是真心的，通常都會願意接受道歉，公司所有人，包含主管階級與員工，都需要從危機中學得教訓。顧客可能會原諒你一次，但是第二次可能就不會原諒你了。

字彙與片語

- crisis ['kraɪsɪs] n. 危機；緊急關頭
- diplomatic [ˌdɪpləˈmætɪk] a. 有外交手腕的；說話辦事得體的；圓滑的

- essential [ɪ'sɛnʃəl] a. 必要的，不可缺的
- acknowledge [ək'nɑlɪdʒ] v. 承認
- specific [spɪ'sɪfɪk] a. 特殊的，特定的
- compensate ['kɑmpən,set] v. 補償，賠償

3. Terminology 財經專業術語

media relations　媒體關係

通過各種媒體和管道來傳播有利於企業發展、產品推廣、品牌影響力的企業相關訊息，如企業文化、管理模式、產品特點、管理者觀點、促銷訊息、市場活動等等。

market research　市場調查

依據一定的理論原則和科學方法，有系統地研究市場商品供需關係，進行資料收集、整理、分析的過程。市場調查為市場預測和經營決策提供準確的情報資料，是市場預測和經營決策的基礎。

the Big Data　大數據

大數據又稱為巨量資料，指的是所涉及的資料量規模龐大，經過專業的收集與管理，可以整理成為對企業經營決策非常有幫助的資訊，伴隨而來的數據收集、數據保存、數據安全、數據分析等，可帶來極大的商業價值和利潤，逐漸成為各行各業的注目焦點。

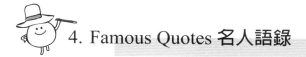

Whoever controls the media, the images, controls the culture.

Allen Ginsberg

控制媒體與影像的人便控制了文化。

艾倫・金斯堡

The creation continues incessantly through the media of man.

Antoni Gaudi

創作隨者人類的媒體不斷進行下去。

安東尼・高第

Digital technology allows us a much larger scope to tell stories that were pretty much the grounds of the literary media.

George Lucas

數位科技給予我們更大的空間來敘述故事，這是在從前只有藝文媒體才有的空間。

喬治・盧卡斯

Smart phones and social media expand our universe. We can connect with others or collect information easier and faster than ever.

Daniel Goleman

智慧型手機和社群媒體開闊了我們的宇宙，我們得以較容易且較快地和他人連結或取得資訊。

丹尼爾・高爾曼

....

I think that more diversity is a good thing, and fresh points of view articulated by people who are committed to excellence in journalism is a beneficial change in the American media landscape.

Al Gore

我認為更多的多樣性是件好事，優秀記者的鮮明立場對於美國媒體整體而言是個好轉變。

艾爾・高爾

Unit 5　Advertisement
廣告

1. Dialogue 實境對話　2-5

A: Do you think we should hire an advertising agency to promote our firm?

B: Our advertising expenses were cut to such an extent that we cannot afford an advertising agency.

A: You mean we do not have the advertising budget?

B: Exactly. Luckily, nowadays, not all advertising media cost a fortune. In fact, many digital media are completely free.

A: How can they sustain themselves if they do not charge the users?

B: They make a fortune from the advertisements on their websites.

A: Are you saying that we should give away the information of our company to digital media?

B: Of course not. Digital media are simply platforms where we put advertising materials, not corporate confidential information.

A: It seems that people from Public Relations should monitor our social media all the time.

B: Not only that. If it is a promotional event, like a marathon game, it probably takes a lot staff and effort. It all depends on the nature of the advertisements or the sales campaign.

A: It sounds quite flexible.

B: And don't forget that many customers we'd like to attract are digital and mobile.

中文翻譯

A： 你認為我們該請一家廣告商來宣傳我們公司嗎？

B： 我們的廣告經費已經被砍了太多，現在已經無法負擔廣告商了。

A： 你的意思是說我們沒有廣告經費了？

B： 沒錯，還好現在不是所有的廣告媒體都要花一大筆費用，事實上，很多數位媒體都完全免費。

A： 他們不收用戶的費用怎麼能生存呢？

B： 他們靠網頁上的廣告就賺一大筆錢了。

A： 你的意思是說我們該提供公司的資訊給這些社群媒體？

B： 當然不是，數位媒體只是讓公司放些廣告素材，而不是公司的機密資訊。

A： 看來公關人員得要隨時檢視我們的社群媒體。

B： 還不只那樣，如果是像馬拉松那樣的宣傳活動，可能就會需要很多的人力，全要看廣告或促銷活動的性質而定。

A： 聽起來相當有彈性。

B： 不要忘了我們所想要吸引的顧客具有數位行動力。

- expense [ɪk'spɛns] n. 費用；價錢；支出
- budget ['bʌdʒɪt] n. 預算；經費
- sustain [sə'sten] v. 承受，承擔
- confidential [ˌkɑnfə'dɛnʃəl] a. 祕密的；機密的
- promotional [prə'moʃən!] a. 促銷的
- flexible ['flɛksəb!] a. 有彈性的

Advertising

The first task in an advertising campaign is to set clear objectives. They can be concrete sales campaigns, such as Christmas sales, or something less concrete, like raising awareness of breast cancer. Once you set your own objectives, you can then consider how to achieve your goals. In a company, this step often involves the advertising budget.

It would be a huge mistake to think that as long as your advertisements attract a great number of interested people the results can be considered very successful. The key in media advertising campaigns is to target a specific audience. In this way, your advertisements can bring about purchasing actions. Your target audience will appreciate the useful information in your advertisements, and nobody will complain about being bombarded by the unsolicited advertising e-mails.

Last but not least, make sure you constantly measure the effectiveness of your advertising. Ask the current customers where they have heard of you and take note of those sources. Pay attention to the feedback of interested customers and follow their suggestions. After all, they make up the main target market, and your products or services are judged by them in the end.

本文翻譯

廣告

　　廣告宣傳活動的第一步驟便是要設立清楚的目標，可以是具體的促銷活動，例如聖誕節特賣，或是較不具體的主題，像是乳癌的衛教宣導活動，在建立個人的目標後，就可以開始思考該要如何達成的方法，這個步驟通常牽涉到廣告經費。

　　如果你認為只要廣告能吸引非常多的人，結果就可以算是很成功，那可就大錯特錯了，在媒體進行廣告宣傳活動，最重要的就是要鎖定特定的族群，這樣子你的廣告才能帶來購買的行動，你鎖定的對象才會珍惜你的廣告的實用訊息，才不會有人抱怨被不想要的廣告信件轟炸。

　　最後而非最不重要的一點是要不斷衡量你廣告的有效性，問一問現有的顧客他們是在哪裡聽到你的訊息，然後記錄下來那些來源，留意感興趣之顧客的回饋，然後遵循他們的建議，畢竟，他們構成了主要的目標市場，而且你的產品或服務最後是由他們來評定的。

字彙與片語

- objective [əb'dʒɛktɪv] n. 目的，目標
- bombard [bɑm'bɑrd] v. 砲擊；轟炸
- unsolicited [ˌʌnsə'lɪsɪtɪd] a. 未經請求的；主動提供的

- measure ['mɛʒɚ] v. 測量；計量
- current ['kɝənt] a. 現時的，當前的

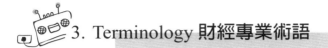

3. Terminology 財經專業術語

shock advertising (shockvertising) 震撼廣告

　　故意藉著不符合社會常規的廣告手段來讓觀眾感到震撼，例如用誇張的廣告台詞與意象，爲的就是想要讓人對其品牌的產品或服務留下深刻印象。有時在推動公共政策，像是宣導反酒駕的活動，也會用此法以求出奇致勝，使人對某議題更加注意。

placement marketing (product placement) 置入性行銷

　　置入性行銷是指刻意將要行銷的產品以巧妙的手法置入既有的媒體，以期藉由既有媒體的曝光率來達成廣告效果。置入性行銷試圖在觀眾沒有防備的情況下，減低觀眾對廣告的抗拒心理，行銷事物和既有媒體不一定相關，一般觀眾也不一定能察覺其爲一種行銷手段。

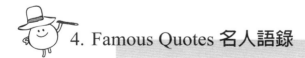

4. Famous Quotes 名人語錄

A good advertisement is one which sells the product without drawing attention to itself.

David Ogilvy

好的廣告能將產品銷售出去，本身卻不會引人注意。

大衛 · 奧格威

Every advertisement should be thought of as a contribution to the complex symbol which is the brand image.

David Ogilvy

每個廣告都應可視爲對品牌形象這個複雜象徵所做的貢獻。

大衛 · 奧格威

As a mom, I know it is my responsibility, and no one else's, to raise my kids. But we have to ask ourselves, what does it mean when so many parents are finding their best efforts undermined by an avalanche of advertisements aimed at our kids.

Michelle Obama

身爲母親，我知道教養我的孩子是我的責任，而非他人的責任，但是我們必須問問自己，爲什麼現在會有這麼多的父母親發現自己付出的心血，都被針對孩子而來的大批廣告暗中破壞了。

蜜雪兒 · 歐巴馬

Promise, large promise, is the soul of an advertisement.

Samuel Johnson

允諾，誇大的允諾，這就是廣告的靈魂。

賽繆爾・詹森

. . . .

I do not read advertisements. I would spend all of my time wanting things.

Franz Kafka

我不看廣告，要不然我整天都會想要買東西。

法蘭茲・卡夫卡

1. Dialogue 實境對話

 2-6

A: How is your English learning going?

B: At the end of this month, I'd like to change my language school.

A: I thought you enjoyed your current English course there very much.

B: In the beginning I did, but as it turned out, it wasn't as good as I'd expected.

A: How so?

B: You know that I signed up for a three month course of advanced conversation.

A: Yes, I remember you said your teacher was from the United States.

B: There were 16 students all together in my class, and we met twice a week in the evening.

A: And then?

B: Two weeks after the course began, some of my fellow students started not to show up.

A: Do you know why?

B: Some said it was because of illness and some had to work overtime. Anyway, new students joined us all of a sudden.

A: Can they catch up with the rest of the class?

B: That's the problem. The class ended up with 22 students of very different levels of speaking ability.

A: Now that the course is going to be ended, are you going to tell the language school about the situation?

B: What for? There is no customer satisfaction survey or anything like that. They don't seem to care at all.

A: Where are you going to learn English then?

B: This time I'll try online English courses.

A: Good luck with that!

中文翻譯

A： 你學英語學得怎麼樣了？

B： 這個月底我想要換語言學校。

A： 我以為你很喜歡現在的英語課程。

B： 剛開始我是很喜歡，但是後來就不如我想的那麼理想。

A： 為什麼呢？

B： 你知道我報名的是三個月的高級會話課程。

A： 對，我記得你告訴我說老師來自美國。

B： 剛開始時我們班共有16個學生，一周兩次，傍晚上課。

A： 然後呢？

B： 開課兩星期後，有些學生開始缺席。

A： 你知道為什麼嗎？

B： 有些說生病了，有些要加班，總之，忽然有新學生加入了。

A： 你跟得上其他同學嗎？

B： 這就是問題所在，結果班上變得有22人，大家的口語能力都參差不齊。

A： 現在既然課程快要結束了，你要告訴語言學校這件事嗎？

B： 何必呢？他們似乎一點也不關心。

A： 那麼你要在哪裡學英語呢？

B： 這次我要試試網路的英語課程。

A： 祝你好運！

字彙與片語

* advanced [əd'vænst] a. 高級的，高等的
* show up 出現，露面；出席
* overtime [,ovɚ'taɪm] adv. 加班
* end up 結果成為；以（壞結果）終結

How to Maintain Customer Loyalty

In almost all businesses, it takes far too much time and effort to earn new customers than to retain old ones. For this practical reason, it makes business sense to do your best to keep your customers coming back. Repeat customers not only contribute to the sales record but also recommend your company and products to their friends and acquaintances.

There are several ways to maintain customer loyalty, and the following strategies are some of the most useful ones. In the first place, having integrity can earn a customer's trust and loyalty. A customer's loyalty cannot be built easily, but an image crisis could completely destroy a customer's trust in an instant. Constantly checking how customers think of your products or services can help improve customer satisfaction. In many companies, a customer satisfaction survey is often used as a tool to gather customer feedback and complaints. From such a survey, you could also find out the reason you may lose customers.

Learning from your customers, especially those who give up on your products, is the best way to know what your strengths and weaknesses are. Meeting customer demand is vital to keeping customers loyal in the competitive market.

如何維持顧客忠誠度

幾乎在所有企業中，要贏得新客戶都比留住舊客戶還要費時耗力得多，因為這個現實的原因，想盡辦法讓顧客再來光顧成為商業必勝之道。忠實顧客不但對業績有貢獻，而且也會將你的公司和產品介紹給他們的朋友和熟人。

要維持客戶忠誠度有幾個方法，以下為幾個最有效的策略：首先，誠信能贏得顧客的信賴與忠誠，顧客的忠心要建立不容易。一次的形象危機可以馬上將其信賴破壞殆盡。經常檢視顧客對你的產品或服務的看法，有助於改善顧客滿意度。很多公司都會使用顧客滿意度調查表來收集顧客的意見與抱怨，藉由這樣的調查表可以找出為何會流失某些顧客的原因。

向顧客學習是知道優缺點的最佳方式，尤其是那些放棄你們公司產品的人。能夠符合顧客的需求是在這個競爭激烈的市場中讓顧客保持忠誠的關鍵。

- retain [rɪ'ten] v. 保留，保持
- contribute [kən'trɪbjut] v. 貢獻
- recommend [ˌrɛkə'mɛnd] v. 推薦，介紹
- integrity [ɪn'tɛgrətɪ] n. 正直；廉正；誠實
- survey [sɚ've] n. 調查；調查報告
- vital ['vaɪt!] a. 極其重要的，必不可少的

3. Terminology 財經專業術語

🥤 customer service　客戶服務

　　客戶服務，是指一種以客戶為導向的價值觀，不僅包含對現有客戶的服務，也包含對潛在客戶的服務，強調服務於企業中的重要性。廣義而言，任何能提高客戶滿意度的內容都屬於客戶服務的範圍之內。

🥤 customer satisfaction　客戶滿意度

　　客戶滿意度，是指客戶體會到的他所實際感知的待遇和所期望的待遇之間的差距。

🥤 customer relationship management (CRM)　客戶關係管理

　　客戶關係管理是一種以「一對一客戶關係理論」為基礎，旨在改善企業與客戶之間關係的新型管理機制。目的是為了滿足每個客戶的特殊需求，來與每個客戶建立聯繫，透過與客戶的聯繫以求了解客戶的不同需求，並在此基礎上，提供客製化服務。通常客戶關係管理包括銷售管理、市場營銷管理、客戶服務系統等方面。

relationship marketing　關係行銷

　　關係行銷是把行銷活動看成是一個企業與消費者、供應商、分銷商、競爭者、政府機構及其他公眾團體發生互動作用的過程，其核心是建立和發展與這些團體的良好關係。

4. Famous Quotes 名人語錄

If people believe they share values with a company, they will stay loyal to the brand.

Howard Schultz

　　如果人們相信他們認同公司的價值，他們就會對品牌維持忠誠度。

霍華德・舒茲

Your most unhappy customers are your greatest source of learning.

Bill Gates

　　你最不滿意的客戶是你學習的最佳來源。

比爾・蓋茲

Get closer than ever to your customers. So close that you tell them what they need well before they realize it themselves.

Steve Jobs

不斷接近你的客戶，直到你可以在他們清楚前告訴他們，他們需要的是什麼。

史蒂夫 · 賈柏斯

....

It is not the employer who pays the wages. Employers only handle the money. It is the customer who pays the wages.

Henry Ford

並非是雇主付給你薪水，雇主只是處理錢而已，付薪水給你的是顧客。

亨利 · 福特

....

The key is to set realistic customer expectations, and then not to just meet them, but to exceed them — preferably in unexpected and helpful ways.

Richard Branson

關鍵在於設定合理的顧客期待值，然後不只要達到期待標準，還要超越——最好是以出其不意而且有效的方式。

李查 · 布蘭森

Chapter 3　Finance

財務

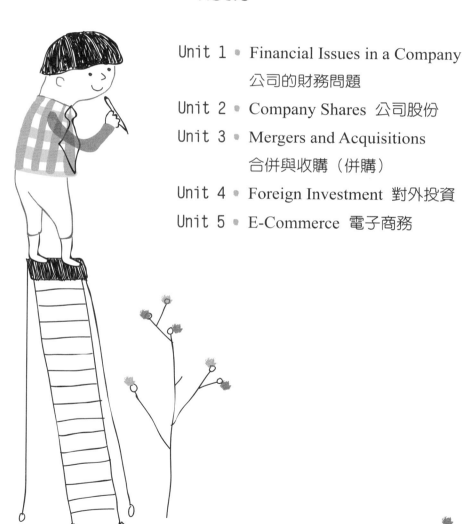

Unit 1 Financial Issues in a Company
公司的財務問題

1. Dialogue 實境對話

 3-1

A: Hey, I see that you are busy doing everything by yourself. Why don't you hire an assistant or a secretary to help you?

B: That would cost our company too much money. On top of the monthly salary, we have to provide insurance.

A: If a multi-tasking assistant can improve the efficiency of our office, the money is very well spent.

B: I know we do have the budget for that, but I always think about how to reduce the costs of our personnel.

A: If you don't mind, we can hire a college graduate to be our intern.

B: But most of the intern applicants have absolutely no experiences of working for any company at all.

A: That's why they are willing to work for us for little or no money. In the end, they gain valuable working experience and our references.

B: By the time I finish training them for their job duties, their time of internship would probably be up already.

A: If so, perhaps you should consider outsourcing. In this age of the Internet, many highly-skilled people are seeking jobs online.

B: How do I groom them for our projects then?

A: Most of our work is task-oriented and can be done under no supervision at all.

B: To save money, I think I'd better learn to become an efficient digital manager.

中文翻譯

A：我看你一個人忙這麼多事，為什麼你不請個助理或秘書來幫你呢？

B：那樣會花公司太多錢，除了每個月的薪水外，我們還必須為他投保。

A：如果這個多功能的助理能改善我們辦公室的效率，這個錢就是花對地方了。

B：我知道我們是有這個預算，但是我總是想降低我們的人事成本。

A：要是你不介意的話，我們可以雇一個大學畢業生來當實習生。

B：但是大多申請實習生的人根本一點工作經驗也沒有。

A：就是因為如此，他們才願意無償或低薪為我們工作，結束後，他們可以獲得價值非凡的工作經驗，還有我們的推薦信。

B：等到我訓練好他們做該做的工作，他們的實習時間可能就已經結束了。

A：既然這樣的話，你應該考慮外包工作，在這個網路時代，很多有高技能的人都在線上尋找工作。

B： 那麼我要怎麼訓練他們做我們的企劃案呢？

A： 我們的工作大多是任務導向的，不需要什麼監督。

B： 為了省錢，我想我最好快學會如何成為有效率的數位經理。

字彙與片語

- multi-tasking ['mʌltɪˌtæskɪŋ] a. 具有多工處理功能的
- personnel [ˌpɝsn'ɛl] n.（總稱）人員，員工
- intern [ɪn'tɝn] n. 實習生
- internship ['ɪntɝnʃɪp] n. 實習職位
- groom [grum] v. 準備
- supervision [ˌsupɚ'vɪʒən] n. 管理；監督

Corporate Financial Transparency

Transparency is characterized by visibility or accessibility of information, especially concerning business practices. In the age of digital technology, corporate financial transparency is a must, and it determines whether a company can succeed or not.

Ever since the financial crisis in 2008, banks and other financial institutions have become more cautious in investing in private businesses. In this competitive climate, financial transparency is essential for small and medium-sized enterprises to attract investment. Aside from banks, shareholders and stakeholders also demand clear financial reports. In the past, there were a number of scandals that some NGOs had dubious cash flow statements and their images were thus seriously shattered.

The credibility of a business depends much on its financial transparency. The investors and the public are smarter than ever and they would not want to see gray zones in the finance of a firm.

本文翻譯

公司財務透明化

透明化的特色是資訊的可見度與可否容易取得的程度，特別是商業行為的相關事項，在這個數位化科技時代，公司財務透明化是不可或缺的，決定了一家公司是否可以成功。

　　自從 2008 年的金融危機以來，銀行和其它金融機構在投資私人企業上變得更加謹慎，在這樣競爭激烈的環境裡，財務透明化對中小企業要吸引投資來說非常重要，除了銀行之外，股東和利害關係人也要求清楚的財務報告，過去曾經發生過一些非營利團體的現金流報告出了問題，他們的形象也因此受到嚴重打擊。

　　企業的可信度要依靠財務透明化，投資者與大眾都比從前還要來得聰明，他們不會很想看見企業財務上出現灰色地帶。

字彙與片語

- transparency [træns'pɛrənsɪ] n. 透明；透明度
- visibility [ˌvɪzə'bɪlətɪ] n. 能見度；明顯性
- accessibility [æk͵sɛsə'bɪlətɪ] n. 易接近，可親；易受影響
- shareholder ['ʃɛr͵holdɚ] n. 股東
- stakeholder ['stek͵holdɚ] n. 利害關係人

3. Terminology 財經專業術語

financial transparency　財務透明度

是指公司財務的公開程度，由於投資者往往根據公司所公布的資訊來決定如何選擇資產組合，因此上市公司的財務透明度是維持市場有效運作的前提。

stakeholder　利害關係人

利害關係人是在一個組織中會影響組織目標或被組織影響的團體或個人，因此，企業的管理者如果想要企業能永續發展，那麼就必須擬定一個能符合各種不同利害關係人的策略才行。

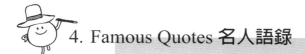

4. Famous Quotes 名人語錄

Beware of little expenses. A small leak will sink a great ship.

Benjamin Franklin

留意微小的支出，一個小裂縫就足以讓一艘大船淹沒。

班傑明‧富蘭克林

It is well enough that people of the nation do not understand our banking and monetary system, for if they did, I believe there would be a revolution before tomorrow morning.

Henry Ford

還好國人不明白我們銀行和金融系統的運作，因為一旦他們明白了，我相信明早之前一定會有一場革命。

亨利·福特

The more entrepreneurs in the world that are getting their ideas financed, the more great companies there are going to be that we can all invest in.

Fred Wilson

世界上有越多人願意投資創業者的創意，就會有越多我們都可以投資的好公司。

佛列得·衛爾森

. . . .

Large companies cannot finance political parties as their shareholders and employees have different political views.

Mikhail Khodorkovsky

大公司無法以金錢支持政黨，因為股東與員工都有不同的政治立場。

米哈伊爾·霍多爾科夫斯基

Unit 2 Company Shares 公司股份

A: What do you think of the employee share incentive plan?

B: Do you mean rewarding employees with shares for their excellent performances?

A: Yes. I read in the newspaper that employees of some companies perform better than others because they are rewarded with shares.

B: That must be a rather big company, right?

A: It seems so. One of those companies is a successful food and beverage business with many chain stores.

B: They can afford giving shares to their employees, but we cannot.

A: Why is that?

B: It is not that easy to let the employees have share ownership.

A: What needs to be done?

B: In order to have a viable employee share incentive plan, many legal and tax problems have to be dealt with first.

A: What else?

B: It also takes a lot of administrative work with the assistance of professionals.

A: That would cost us lots of money.

B: Most important of all, do our employees really want it?

A: From my point of view, they would rather have increased year-end bonuses than company shares. Cash is always much more useful to them than anything else.

B: I couldn't agree more.

中文翻譯

A： 你認為員工分紅入股制度好嗎？

B： 你的意思是說讓員工持有公司的股權來獎勵他們的優良表現？

A： 是的，我在報紙上讀到說有些公司的員工表現傑出，因為他們能分紅入股。

B： 一定是間相當大型的公司吧？

A： 好像是，其中一家是非常成功的大型餐飲連鎖店。

B： 他們能夠負擔得起讓員工分紅入股，我們不能。

A： 為什麼呢？

B： 讓員工持有股權不是那麼容易。

A： 有什麼要做的呢？

B： 為了要使員工分紅入股制度能運作正常，首先要處理很多法律和稅務問題。

A： 還有呢？

B： 還需要很多行政工作，以及專業人士的協助。

A： 那會需要很大的一筆花費。

B： 更重要的一點是，我們的員工真的想要嗎？

A： 依我看來，比起持股，他們寧可要提高年終獎金，對他們來說，現金總是比其它東西都來得有用。

B： 我完全同意你的看法。

字彙與片語

- incentive [ɪn'sɛntɪv] a. 鼓勵的，獎勵的
- ownership ['onɚˌʃɪp] n. 所有權
- viable ['vaɪəb!] a. 可實行的
- administrative [əd'mɪnəˌstretɪv] a. 管理的；行政的
- year-end bonus 年終獎金

The Employee Share Incentive Scheme

Recently, we have often heard that some companies outperform others because their employers reward employees with company shares. Does the employee share incentive scheme really give employees the pride of ownership and increase their productivity? What are some of the issues involved in giving employee shares?

While some employees really can be motivated by company shares, many prefer cash because they can use it right away. Not all staff can be retained longer in the corporation because of the shares they hold. As we all know, most shares can be purchased and sold very easily. For all the legal and tax issues involved, lawyers and accountants have to be hired for the planning of share incentives. Besides, annual shareholder meetings have to be held, where corporate financial statements must be disclosed, and certain control of the company might be lost as a result.

The benefits of employee share incentive plans are attractive to many employers, but as seen above, quite a lot of work and cost will be required in the whole process. Striking the right balance determines the success of the outcome of implementing employee share schemes.

員工分紅入股制度

　　最近我們經常聽說有的公司表現傑出，因為他們的員工表現優良的人就能分紅入股，到底員工分紅入股制度是否真能帶給員工持有股權的榮譽感，並且增加生產力呢？讓員工入股到底牽涉到哪些問題呢？

　　雖然有些員工真的能夠因為持有股權而受到激勵，但是很多員工還是比較喜歡現金，因為馬上能使用。並非所有的員工都會因為持股而在公司待得久一點，眾所周知，大多數的股票可以輕易地轉手，為了解決法律和稅務問題，還要雇用律師和會計師來規劃員工分紅入股制度，除此之外，還必須舉行年度股東會議並公布公司財務報告，公司的部分控制權可能會因此而喪失。

　　員工分紅入股制度的益處對很多雇主來說非常吸引人，不過由以上幾點可知，整個過程需要大量的操作成本，在這當中是否能求得一個真正平衡點，決定了實施員工分紅入股制度的結果是否能夠成功。

字彙與片語

- scheme [skim] n. 計畫；方案
- productivity [ˌprodʌkˈtɪvətɪ] n. 生產力；生產率
- motivate [ˈmotəˌvet] v. 刺激；激發

- disclose [dɪs'kloz] v. 揭發；透露；公開
- implement ['ɪmplə,mɛnt] v. 實施；執行

3. Terminology 財經專業術語

share (stock)　股票

　　股票是股份證書的簡稱，是股份公司為籌集資金而發行給股東，作為持股憑證並藉以取得股息和紅利的一種有價證券。每股股票都代表股東對企業擁有一個基本單位的所有權，這種所有權是一種綜合權利，如參加股東大會、投票表決、參與公司的重大決策、收取股息或分享紅利等。同一類別的每一份股票所代表的公司所有權是相等的，每個股東所擁有的公司所有權份額的大小，取決於其持有的股票數量占公司總股本的比重。股票是股份公司資本的構成部分，可以轉讓、買賣或作價抵押，是資本市場的主要長期信用工具，但不能要求公司返還其出資。股東與公司之間的關係不是債權債務關係，股東是公司的所有者，以其出資份額為限對公司負有限責任，承擔風險，分享收益。

employee stock ownership trust (ESOT)　員工持股信託

　　即員工成為所服務企業的股東。員工入股的定義有廣義和狹義之別：狹義的員工入股指公司為使員工取得所屬公司股票而提供各種便利制度；廣義的員工入股則為員工持有公司的股票為公司依獎勵、斡旋、援助等方法，做為推進公司的方針或政策的總稱。

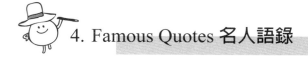

Wide diversification is only required when investors do not understand what they are doing.

Warren Buffett

大量的多元化只有在投資者不明白他們在做什麼的時候才會需要。

華倫・巴菲特

....

Why not invest your assets in the companies you really like? As Mae West said, 'Too much of a good thing can be wonderful'.

Warren Buffett

為什麼不將你的資產投資於你真正喜歡的公司？就如同馬耶・維斯特所說：「好東西多擁有一點總是件好事。」

華倫・巴菲特

....

If a business does well, the stock eventually follows.

Warren Buffett

如果一家企業經營得好，股票自然就會跟著看好。

華倫・巴菲特

....

Our favorite holding period is forever.

Warren Buffett

我們的最佳持股時間是永遠。

華倫 · 巴菲特

· ·

When buying shares, ask yourself, would you buy the whole company?

Rene Rivkin

買股票的時候問一問你自己，你會想買下這整間公司嗎？

瑞內 · 里維金

Mergers and Acquisitions
合併與收購（併購）

1. Dialogue 實境對話 3-3

A: Have you received an e-mail from the head office in America saying that our company will soon be merged?

B: Yes, I just got that e-mail. To me, it seems that our company is going to be acquired by another company soon.

A: What's the difference between a merger and an acquisition?

B: When two companies of equal sizes are joined, it is called a merger. In our case, it's more likely that we are going to be taken over by a much bigger company in an acquisition.

A: Will we be able to keep our positions?

B: Everyone is wondering about that issue.

A: No information about this was stated in the e-mail I received. Maybe the people in the head office don't have the answers yet.

B: In the e-mail I got, it says that the general manager for Asia will visit us sometime next week and talk to us about the possible new packages if we continue working here.

A: Are you going to stay?

B: I would if I could still be the sales manager and get the same salary.

中文翻譯

A： 你收到了美國總公司寄來的電子郵件，說我們公司快被合併了嗎？

B： 我剛收到了，依我看來，我們公司快被另一家公司收購了。

A： 合併與收購有什麼不同呢？

B： 當兩家大小相似的公司結合在一起，稱為合併，在我們的情況，我們比較像是會被另一家比我們大得多的公司收購。

A： 我們的工作保得住嗎？

B： 大家都在想這個問題。

A： 我收到的電子郵件中沒有提到這方面訊息，或許總公司的人也不清楚答案。

B： 我收到的電子郵件說亞洲區的總經理下星期會來看我們，並且和我們談留下來工作可能有的新薪資福利。

A： 你會留下來嗎？

B： 如果能繼續當業務經理並且領同樣的薪水，我就會留下來。

 字彙與片語

- merger [mɝdʒɚ] n.（公司等的）合併
- acquisition [ˌækwəˈzɪʃən] n.（公司等的）收購
- state [stet] v. 陳述；聲明；說明
- head office 總公司；總部

- package ['pækɪdʒ] n. 一組事物、交易（計畫、建議等）

2. Article 文章

How to Avoid Corporate Culture Clashes in a Merger

A merger is often compared to a marriage in which both sides bring in different values and practices. Corporate culture clashes can easily happen and might hinder overall performance and productivity. In order to minimize these damages, it is essential to analyze both corporate cultures carefully.

It is hard to assess the qualities of a corporate culture, but it is vital in understanding the core values of the new firm. One key strategy is not to change everything. Usually, it is the case that one company is more dominating than the other. It pays to preserve certain aspects of the smaller entity. In the meantime, make the expectations clear to all employees and allow them enough time to adjust to the new transition. Good communication between headquarters and branch offices can facilitate the merger.

It is worthwhile to study the other company carefully before the merger, and always remember that it takes time to have the employees settle in and allow a merger to actually happen.

本文翻譯

如何在合併中避免企業文化衝突

合併通常被比喻成結婚，雙方都會帶來不同的價值與作法。企業文化的衝突很容易發生，很可能會阻礙整體的表現與生產力，為了要減低這些傷害，仔細分析雙方的企業文化是非常重要的。

要衡量一個企業文化的質量，有一定的難度，但是一定要去了解新公司的核心價值，關鍵在於不要去改變所有的作法，通常一方會比另一方強勢，保留較小那一實體的某些特質會帶來好處，同時，讓所有員工清楚明白預期目標，讓他們有足夠時間來適應新的轉變，總公司和分公司之間的良好溝通可以讓合併更順利。

在合併之前值得花時間仔細研究對方，要永遠記得，要使員工安頓下來與合併真正發生，都是需要時間的。

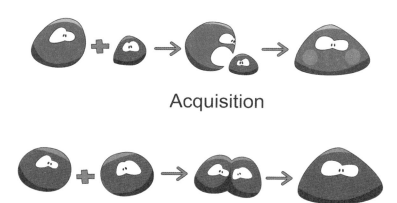

Acquisition

Merger

- clash [klæʃ] n. 衝突；不協調
- hinder ['hɪndɚ] v. 妨礙；阻礙
- dominating ['dɑməˌnetɪŋ] a. 強勢的
- preserve [prɪ'zɝv] v. 保護；維護；維持
- entity ['ɛntətɪ] n. 實體
- facilitate [fə'sɪləˌtet] v. 使容易；促進；幫助

3. Terminology 財經專業術語

mergers and acquisitions (M&A)　合併與收購（併購）

　　是策略管理、企業財務的術語，指不用創建子公司或合資公司的方式，而是通過購買及合併不同公司或類似的實體，以幫助企業在其領域、行業、產地等方面快速成長。實際操作中，「合併」以及「收購」之間的區別越來越小，儘管經常被交替使用，「合併」和「收購」還是略有區別：當一個公司收購了另一個公司並以新業主自稱，這項購買被稱爲「收購」，從法律上來說，目標公司不再存在，買家已經吞食了賣家的生意，而買家的股票仍舊在正常交易；「合併」嚴格說起來是兩個公司同意合成一個公司，擁有權和經營權都合而爲一，這樣的行爲可以更準確地被稱做「平等兼併」，通常這兩家公司規模相當，兩家的股票都下市，取而代之的是新公司的股票發行。

hostile takeover　惡意收購

又稱「敵意併購」、「強制收購」，指收購公司在未經目標公司董事會允許，不管對方是否同意的情況下，所進行的收購活動。當事雙方採用各種攻防策略完成收購行為，並希望取得控制性股權，成為大股東。當中，雙方強烈的對抗性是其基本特點，除非目標公司的股票流通量高，否則收購困難。惡意收購可能併發突襲收購。

4. Famous Quotes 名人語錄

Any successful company in the valley gets acquisition offers and has to decide whether or not to take them.

Marc Andreessen

所有矽谷成功的公司都會收到收購的要求，都必須要做出是否要接受的決定。

馬克・安德森

. . . .

We continue to look at accretive and synergistic acquisitions both in the domestic as well as international markets. Our emphasis, thus, will be on strategic acquisitions, and we will not be doing it just for the sake of making our name bigger.

Adi Godrej

我們繼續審視增值與合作的收購，國內與國外市場皆可，因此我們強調的是策略上的收購，而且我們的目的不是只為了讓自己更出名。

阿迪・高蒂瑞傑

. . . .

As I have seen with a lot of companies I have covered, acquisition interest can be a heady experience, and not always in a good way.

Kara Swisher

在我所看到的很多我談及的公司當中，收購的興趣可能會讓人感到很陶醉，但卻不一定是件好事。

卡拉・斯維薛爾

. . . .

Seeking an acquisition from the start is more than just bad advice for an entrepreneur. For the entrepreneur it leads to short term tactical decisions rather than company-building decisions and in my view often reduces the probability of success.

Vinod Khosla

對創業家來說，尋找收購一開始就是個糟糕到不行的建議，收購帶給創業家的是短期策略性的決定，而不是關於建立公司的決定，在我看來，這麼做經常會降低成功獲利的可能性。

維諾蒂・寇斯拉

Unit 4   Foreign Investment
對外投資

1. Dialogue 實境對話

3-4

A: They say that Facebook is thinking about setting up a data center in Changhua, Taiwan.

B: That sounds very promising, but why would they be that interested in investing in Taiwan?

A: It is the proximity to China that is strategically important to Facebook.

B: What are some other reasons?

A: Facebook is keen on Taiwan because of the low costs of water and electricity.

B: I see.

A: Plus, the relatively low taxes and labor costs in Taiwan.

B: Then we can expect Facebook to bring quite a lot of employment opportunities to Taiwan.

A: I wouldn't hold my breath for that. Not all international investments hire many local people.

B: I can imagine that such a gigantic data plant will take a lot of energy to maintain and cause serious air pollution to the environment.

A: Water pollution as well.

B: How do the people in Changhua feel about this overseas investment?

A: The local government, at least, is embracing the investment plan and hopes it will attract more international investments.

中文翻譯

A： 聽說臉書公司正考慮在台灣的彰化設立數據中心。

B： 聽起來很不錯，但是他們為什麼會對在台灣投資那麼感興趣呢？

A： 台灣距離中國很近，這點在戰略上對臉書公司來說非常重要。

B： 還有其它什麼原因嗎？

A： 臉書公司因為水費與電費較低而對台灣感興趣。

B： 我明白了。

A： 還有，台灣的稅務與勞工薪資都相當低。

B： 那麼臉書公司應該會為台灣帶來不少的就業機會。

A： 這點我不敢奢望，並非所有國際投資都會雇用很多當地人。

B： 我可以想見這樣大型的數據中心會需要靠很多的能源來維護，會對環境造成很嚴重的空氣汙染。

A： 還有水汙染。

B： 彰化當地人對這項海外投資感到怎麼樣？

A： 至少當地政府對這項投資計劃非常期待，他們希望這項投資能吸引更多的國際投資。

- promising ['pramisiŋ] a. 有希望的，有前途的，大有可為的

- proximity [prak'simətɪ] n. 接近，鄰近；親近

- keen [kin] a. 熱心的，熱衷的

- relatively ['rɛlətɪvlɪ] adv. 相對地，比較而言；相當

- gigantic [dʒaɪ'gæntɪk] a. 巨大的，龐大的

Foreign Investment

Currently, there is a trend toward globalization and wherever you go, you can find chain stores and offices of large, multinational firms. With the Internet, the accessibility and popularity of foreign investments have increased more than ever.

There are two types of foreign investment: direct foreign investment and indirect foreign investment. The former happens when companies make physical investments in another country. For example, a huge firm decides to branch out or a manufacturing business wants to set up or to buy a plant overseas. Usually such a physical investment is attracted by the local resources, low tax, or labor costs. Sometimes, small firms might be purchased by foreign companies for their special technology, products, and clients. Foreign investment in another country is often regarded as a positive sign of creating more employment and economic prosperity. On the other hand, indirect foreign investment takes the form of buying foreign currencies, stocks or bonds in banks or financial institutions. Generally speaking, indirect investment is not as stable as direct investment.

With the increasing popularity of trade deals between countries, we often can have investments in a great variety of countries. By opening up branches or factories outside of our country, we have also opened up the door to future economic growth.

本文翻譯

對外投資

目前有一股全球化的趨勢，無論去到哪裡，都可以看見大型跨國公司的連鎖店和分公司，再加上網路，對外投資較從前更為方便且普及。

有兩種對外投資：對外直接與對外間接投資。對外直接投資是指公司在別的國家進行有形的投資，例如，一家大型公司決定要在海外設立分公司，或製造商要在海外設廠或購買工廠，通常這種有形的投資是因為受到當地資源、繳稅或勞力低廉吸引而來，有時候小型公司可能會因為特別的技術、產品、客戶，被外國公司收購，在海外投資通常被視為是正面的徵兆，可以創造更多的就業，使經濟繁榮；而對外間接投資是在銀行或金融機構購買外國的貨幣、股票、債券。通常來說，對外間接投資不如對外直接投資那麼穩定。

國與國之間的貿易交易日益普及，我們經常可以在許多不同國家進行投資，藉著在海外開分公司與工廠，我們同時也開啓了未來經濟成長之門。

字彙與片語

- trend [trɛnd] n. 趨勢，傾向
- former ['fɔrmɚ] a. （兩者中）前者的

- currency ['kɜ·ənsɪ] n. 貨幣
- bond [bɑnd] n. 債券，公債
- stable ['steb!] a. 穩定的

3. Terminology 財經專業術語

foreign investment　對外投資

又稱國際投資（International Investment），或海外投資（Overseas Investment），是指跨國公司等國際投資主體，將其擁有的貨幣資本或產業資本，通過跨國界流動和營運，以實現價值增值的經濟行為。

foreign direct investment & foreign indirect investment 對外直接投資與對外間接投資

以投資經營權有無為依據，對外投資可分為對外直接投資（Foreign Direct Investment）和對外間接投資（Foreign Indirect Investment），直接投資與間接投資的區別：基本區分所在是投資者是否能有效地控制作為投資對象的外國企業，即對國外企業的有效控制權。對外直接投資的性質和投資過程比對外間接投資複雜，投資者獲取收益的性質和風險不同。

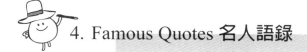

4. Famous Quotes 名人語錄

If you want to attract more investment, foreign investment, more talent, more business, I think having some level of certainty that the business environment respects, those who have been your partners for a long time, is important.

Louis R. Chenevert

如果你想要吸引更多的投資，外國的投資，還有更多的人才、更多的企業，我認爲確保商業環境對長久合作夥伴的尊敬，這一點是很重要的。

路意士 · 艾 · 徹内凡特

....

America still has the right stuff to thrive. We still have the most creative, diverse, innovative culture and open society — in a world where the ability to imagine and generate new ideas with speed and to implement them through global collaboration is the most important competitive advantage.

Thomas Friedman

美國還是有本事繁榮起來，我們的文化還是最有創意，最多元，最創新，我們的社會很開放——在這樣的環境中，有想像力，能快速開發新點子，並且透過全球合作將這些點子付諸實行，這就是最重要的競爭優勢。

湯馬士 · 費列德曼

China should be developing through the various foreign investments it receives. I hope for its level-headed and rational understanding that anything to discourage that is a disservice to itself.

Yoshihiko Noda

中國應該早就能靠各種的外國投資發展起來，我希望他們能有冷靜且理智的想法，明白任何對這個趨勢的阻礙都是對自己的不利。

野田佳彥

. . . .

Everybody you talk to about insurance says the insurance market has become a lot more vibrant as a result of lifting, allowing the foreign direct investment.

John W. Snow

所有與你談論保險業的人都會說，保險市場已經因為解除限制，容許外國直接投資，發展得更加蓬勃。

約翰・懷・史諾

. . . .

Creating a better world requires teamwork, partnerships, and collaboration, as we need an entire army of companies to work together to build a better world within the next few decades. This means corporations must embrace the benefits of cooperating with one another.

Simon Mainwaring

要創造一個更好的世界需要團隊合作、合夥關係、同心協力，就如同我們需要與很多公司一起合作，才能在接下來幾十年內建立一個更好的世界，這表示企業必須擁抱互相合作的好處。

賽門・麥瓦菱

Unit 5   E-Commerce
電子商務

1. Dialogue 實境對話   🎧 3-5

A: Have you thought about selling your products online?

B: Do you really think that someone would buy our mechanical components on the Internet?

A: Why not? Many people surf the Internet almost every day and order all sorts of things.

B: I've been in this industry for a long time, and I've never seen any online purchases in the market. Most customers have to see and feel the metal products before they can make buying decisions.

A: In the past, nobody would believe that consumers would buy electronic products like vacuum cleaners from the Internet, but now it is very popular to do so.

B: I don't think any of my customers would feel comfortable submitting their billing data online. The key issue with e-commerce is cyber security, don't you think?

A: You are absolutely right. In fact, quite a few companies hire many IT experts to fight against hackers who try to break into their systems for customer information.

B: Since so many companies use the Internet to operate their businesses, it must mean that e-commerce is very profitable.

A: E-commerce is trendy because it's fast. What's more, nowadays, it is mobile, too.

B: What do you mean?

A: With smart phones, customers can place their orders wherever they are, whenever they want.

B: Sounds like I should immediately hire a tech specialist to design an interface for mobile devices.

A: Think about all the business opportunities you will miss if you don't start now!

中文翻譯

A： 你有沒有想過在網路上賣你們的產品？

B： 你真的以為有人會想要網購我們的機械零件？

A： 為什麼不會呢？很多人每天上網買各式各樣的東西。

B： 我做這一行很久了，從來沒看過有人從網路訂貨，大部分客戶都要先看過、摸過這些金屬產品，才能決定是否要買。

A： 從前沒有人相信會有人上網買吸塵器等家電產品，但是現在很流行這麼做。

B： 我想我的客戶不會有人願意在網路上傳個人付費的資料，關於電子商務最重要的是網路安全問題，你不這麼認為嗎？

A： 你說的非常正確，事實上很多公司都會雇用很多電腦工程師來對付企圖駭進系統，竊取客戶資料的駭客。

B： 既然有很多人使用網路來經營企業，代表電子商務一定是有利可圖。

A： 電子商務因為快捷而流行起來，還有一點，現在也非常機動。

B： 你的意思是？

A： 因為智慧型手機，消費者可以隨時隨地下訂單。

B： 聽起來我似乎該馬上雇用科技專員來設計行動裝置的平台。

A： 想想看你如果不馬上開始會錯過多少的商機！

字彙與片語

- e-commerce 電子商務
- vacuum cleaner （真空）吸塵器
- cyber security 網路安全
- hacker [ˋhækɚ] n. 駭客
- trendy [ˋtrɛndɪ] a. 時髦的；流行的

E-Commerce

In the recent years, e-commerce has evolved quite a lot and at a dramatic speed. Originally, only giant companies dominated the market. Right now, almost all products can be purchased online and delivered to your doorstep. Even the smallest private businesses seem to have a presence on the Internet.

Managing online stores takes a lot of strategies, including the initial planning, maintenance and improvement. Your web presence has to allow customers to navigate easily. The information of products must be clearly visible. Customers have to be able to set up their accounts and place their orders without trouble. The security concern must be taken care of by IT specialists. To maintain customer satisfaction, constant updates are required. Technological improvements brought about smart phones and other mobile devices, and that means companies should also have mobile accesses.

In 2015, Amazon opened its first physical shop in Seattle and has attracted many customers. This connection of real and cyber stores is a good example of the modern living way of O2O, Online to Offline. Many book buyers can order books online and pick up their books in the physical bookstore, which also makes exchanging books very easy. Of course, loyal customers continue voicing their feedback on the Internet to Amazon. In other words, e-commerce has integrated into traditional ways of doing business.

電子商務

最近幾年，電子商務進展速度驚人，原先只有大型公司在主導市場，現在，幾乎所有產品都可以於網路上買到並宅配到家，甚至似乎連最小的私人企業在網路上也有資訊。

要管理網路商家需要很多策略，包含最初的計劃，還有維護與改善，你的網路內容必須要能讓顧客輕易瀏覽，產品的資訊必須要非常清楚明白，顧客要能輕鬆設立帳號來下訂單，資訊工程師必須要顧好安全問題，為了要維持顧客的滿意程度，內容要經常更新。科技進步帶來了智慧型手機與其它行動裝置，公司也因此要能在行動配備上跟進。

在 2015 年，亞馬遜公司於西雅圖開了第一家實體店面，吸引了很多顧客上門，這樣的實體與網路商店的連結，是現今一個結合線上與線下生活的好例子，很多買書的人可以在網路上訂書，然後在實體書店取書，這樣換書也變得很容易。當然，忠實顧客還是繼續在網路上將他們的意見反應給亞馬遜公司。換句話說，電子商務已經融入傳統做生意的方式。

字彙與片語

- evolve [ɪˈvɑlv] v. 發展，展開
- initial [ɪˈnɪʃəl] a. 開始的，最初的
- maintenance [ˈmentənəns] n. 維持，保持
- navigate [ˈnævəˌget] v. 航行；駕駛
- integrate [ˈɪntəˌgret] v. 融入，結合

3. Terminology 財經專業術語

Electronic Commerce (E-Commerce)　電子商務

　　是指利用電腦與網路，將整個交易過程電子化、數位化、網路化，人們不再是面對面，看著實際的物品，使用紙鈔進行買賣，而是透過網路上琳瑯滿目的商品訊息，完善的物流配送系統來下單，並且藉著方便安全的金額結算系統來進行交易。

The Internet of Things　物聯網

　　物聯網的概念是在 1999 年提出的，它的定義很簡單：把所有物品透過訊息感測設備與互聯網連接起來，實現智能化識別和管理。物聯網通過智能感應、識別技術，廣泛在網絡的融合應用，被稱為繼計算機、互聯網之後，世界資訊產業發展的第三次浪潮。

Brands will increasingly handle their own e-commerce and rely less and less on local distribution partners. Why should they give away their profit margins?

Natalie Massenet

品牌公司會越來越仰賴他們自己的電子商務,而非地方經銷商,他們何必要將利潤讓別人賺走呢?

娜塔莉・馬賽內特

....

Communications is at the heart of e-commerce and community.

Meg Whitman

溝通是電子商務和社群的中心。

美格・懷特曼

....

Amazon.com strives to be the e-commerce destination where consumers can find and discover anything they want to buy online.

Jeff Bezos

亞馬遜網購公司致力於成為電子商務的最終目的地,讓消費者能夠在這裡找到、發現所有他們在網路上想買的物品。

傑夫・貝索

Yahoo is in everything from pets to old people to finance to communications to e-commerce and more, and I really thrive on that.

Jerry Yang

Yahoo 所賣的東西包含寵物類、銀髮族用品、金融服務、通訊業、電子商務，還有更多更多的產品與服務，我真的感到很得意。

楊致遠

....

Leadership in telecommunications is also essential, since we are now in the age of e-commerce.

Michael Oxley

領導力在電子通訊業也很重要，因為我們現在處於電子商務時代。

麥可・歐克斯里

Chapter 4 Human Resources and Organization

人力資源與組織

Unit 1 Recruitment
招募新進員工

1. Dialogue 實境對話 4-1

A: What makes you think you are the right candidate for the position?

B: Based on my educational background and working experiences, I am no doubt the most suitable person for the job.

A: Why did you leave your last company?

B: My last company was merged into another large firm, and due to that I lost the job.

A: Why have you changed jobs so frequently?

B: Once, the company went bankrupt all of a sudden, and at another time the position was taken over by a college graduate, who was paid much less than me.

A: Are you a good team player?

B: On any team in my previous companies, I often played the role of an excellent team leader.

A: Are you good at dealing with stress?

B: Yes, I would say my EQ is quite high. Positive stress often pushes me to accomplish my tasks in time.

A: We have high expectations of our employees. Do you think you can get used to that?

B: That would not be any problem at all. I do have high expectations of myself and like to face challenges. What I am looking for is a job that can help me grow.

A: How much money do you want?

B: Any pay above TWD 30000 would be fine to me.

A: You can start to work here next Monday, but bear in mind, the probation period is three months.

B: Thank you very much.

中文翻譯

A：為什麼你自認是這個職位的最佳人選？

B：從我的學經歷看來，我無疑是做這工作的最適合的人。

A：你為何離開上一家公司？

B：我上家公司被另一家公司合併了，因此我丟了工作。

A：為什麼你換工作如此頻繁？

B：有一次，公司忽然倒閉了，一次，我的職位被一個大學畢業生搶走了，他的薪水比我低很多。

A：你在團隊中表現很好嗎？

B：在我先前公司的任何團隊中，我經常扮演團隊領導人物，表現很好。

A：你的抗壓性高嗎？

B：很高，我認為我的情緒商數很高，正向壓力常常讓我能及時完成工作。

A： 我們對員工的要求很高，你覺得你適應得了嗎？

B： 我不會有任何問題，我對自己的要求很高，喜歡自我挑戰，我要找的是能幫助我成長的工作。

A： 你的期待薪水是多少？

B： 三萬元以上台幣都可以。

A： 那麼下星期一你可以開始來上班，不過要記住，試用期為三個月。

B： 非常感謝。

字彙與片語

- recruitment [rɪˈkrutmənt] n. 人才招募
- candidate [ˈkændədet] n. 求職應徵者
- background [ˈbækˌɡraʊnd] n. 出身背景；（包括學歷在內的）經歷
- bankrupt [ˈbæŋkrʌpt] a. 破產的；有關破產的
- accomplish [əˈkɑmplɪʃ] v. 完成，實現，達到
- probation [proˈbeʃən] n. 試用；見習

Recruitment

If you are a captain of a ship, you want to have the right crewmen aboard. These days, many employers use an aptitude test to choose the most suitable candidates. What constitutes an aptitude test differs in all positions of various industries, but it seems to center on the ability to work well with others.

Whether you are looking for someone to work in the sales department or not, this candidate should be able to represent the company. If the employees genuinely like people, in general, they will be naturally friendly when facing customers. They will be able to work much better with their coworkers and contribute more to the collaborative work of their teams. Attributes like this cannot be measured in a test of professional skills, such as computer skills. That is why many companies right now use an aptitude test, as well as interviews, in their new staff recruitments.

Most of the newcomers have a probation period, like three months, to test if they are really capable of the requirements of the positions. During this probation, the employer and the new employee observe each other to see if they are compatible. It is usually a time for the new members of the company to demonstrate their abilities of professionalism and social skills.

招募新進員工

如果你是一艘船的船長，你會希望船員都為合適人選，現今很多雇主會使用性向測驗來挑選最合適的人才，性向測驗的內容依不同產業的職位而有些許差異，但是似乎都圍繞著與他人共事的良好能力。

無論你是否在尋找業務部門的員工，這個候選人都必須要能代表公司：如果員工個性喜歡與人相處，就會用真心友善對待客戶，他們會與同事相處得更愉快，在團隊中更能與人合作，有更多的貢獻。像這類的特質不能像電腦技能那樣用某項專業技能測試來評量，因此現在很多公司使用性向測驗加上面試來招募新進員工。

大部分的新進員工有三個月那樣的試用期來測試他們的能力是否真的符合這份工作的要求，在試用期內，公司的雇主和新進員工會彼此觀察，看看是否合得來，通常這是能讓新進員工表現專業能力和社交技巧的一段時間。

字彙與片語

- aptitude ['æptə,tjud] n. 傾向，習性；天賦
- represent [,rɛprɪ'zɛnt] v. 作為……的代表
- genuinely ['dʒɛnjʊɪnlɪ] adv. 真誠地；誠實地
- attribute ['ætrə,bjut] n. 特性，特質
- compatible [kəm'pætəb!] a. 能共處的

3. Terminology 財經專業術語

recruitment　招募甄選

　　招募甄選是指尋找、篩選及錄用適當人選出任組織職位空缺的過程。

talent retention　人才保留

　　人才保留是指企業運用某種激勵方式來讓人才不流失，能夠繼續為公司效力。

human resources　人力資源

　　人力資源是指一定時期內組織中的人所擁有的，能夠被企業所用，且對價值創造起貢獻作用的教育、能力、技能、經驗、體力等的總稱。

human resource management　人力資源管理

　　是指企業的一系列人力資源政策以及相應的管理活動，這些活動主要包括企業人力資源戰略的制定、員工的招募與培訓、績效管理、薪酬管理、員工流動管理、員工關係管理、員工安全與健康管理等。

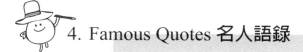

4. Famous Quotes 名人語錄

But even race-neutral policies and recruitment efforts designed to achieve greater diversity are, in the end, not race neutral.

Adam Schiff

但是即使是種族中立的政策和爲了招募更多元化新進員工所做的努力，最終都無法達到種族中立的目的。

亞當・雪夫

Let's face it: Engineering companies in general have more men than women. Google has tried really hard to recruit women. On the other hand, we have a standard. Google tries to recruit the best engineers.

Susan Wojcicki

讓我們承認這一點：大部分工程公司都雇用較多的男性員工，較少的女性員工。谷歌眞的一直以來都很努力招募女性新進員工，然而，我們有一定的標準，谷歌希望要招募的對象是最佳工程師。

蘇珊・沃基可克

Many dotcoms recruited people from existing companies who were quite experienced in finance, marketing, distribution and other disciplines but not necessarily experienced in the Web culture.

John Patrick

很多網路公司招募的新進員工爲別家既有公司的財務、行銷、分配等領域的資深專家，但是他們卻不一定在網路文化這方面有經驗。

約翰 · 派翠克

. . . .

LinkedIn is increasingly becoming a very strong place for companies to develop their talent plans, their recruitment plans, and so there are ways in which we can track some of the momentum there.

Jeff Weiner

LinkedIn 越來越成爲公司開發人才和進行新員工招募計劃的有效平台，所以我們應該好好善用在那邊的氣勢。

傑夫 · 維納爾

Unit 2　Corporate Culture
企業文化

1. Dialogue 實境對話　4-2

A: Did you know that most European companies will pay settlement costs to relocate the staff and their families?

B: Really? How nice is that!

A: It is part of their corporate culture to look after their employees and their families.

B: No wonder European employees can afford to live in good neighborhoods and send their children to expensive private schools in Taiwan.

A: What is it like in Taiwanese companies?

B: In contrast to that, many Taiwanese employees are forced to take up positions in China or they will be demoted.

A: After working abroad for a period of time, employees of European companies can apply to work in their own countries as consultants, or whatever suits them, in the same company.

B: That's very thoughtful. Otherwise, the employees could not give their 100 percent to the company, wondering what the future for them and their families would be.

A: Most European companies have long-term plans for human resources.

B: I wish my Taiwanese company could offer the same to us. I know many Taiwanese people who have worked for several years in China who want to come back, but their old positions in Taiwan are already taken by others.

A: Treating employees well is valued in the corporate culture of European companies. In this respect, the employees are treated like family members and are therefore, willing to contribute their best to their companies.

中文翻譯

A： 你知道大部分的歐洲公司會給員工和他們家庭因工作遷居的費用嗎？

B： 真的嗎？那真是太好了。

A： 照顧員工與他們家庭是他們企業文化之一。

B： 怪不得歐洲員工在台灣可以住得起好社區，送得起他們的小孩去上昂貴的私校。

A： 台灣公司的情形是怎麼樣的呢？

B： 相較之下，很多台灣員工都被迫到中國大陸工作，不然的話，他們會被降職。

A： 歐洲企業的員工可以在海外工作一段時間後，申請回到自己國家在同一公司當顧問或其它適合的職位。

B： 那真是體貼，要不然的話，員工可就無法全心全力為公司工作，因為不時在煩惱自己和家人的未來。

A： 大部分歐洲公司的人力資源部門有長程的計劃。

B： 真希望台灣企業也能提供如此的待遇，據我所知，很多在中國大陸工作很多年的台灣人想要回來，但是他們在台灣原有的職位卻已經被別人占據了。

A： 善待員工為歐洲公司的企業文化所重視，在這一方面，員工如同家庭成員那般受到照顧，因此會盡力對公司做貢獻。

字彙與片語

- corporate ['kɔrpərɪt] a. 團體的；公司的
- relocate [ri'loket] v.（將……）重新安置
- demote [dɪ'mot] v. 降級
- thoughtful ['θɔtfəl] a. 體貼的，考慮周到的
- respect [rɪ'spɛkt] n. 方面，著眼點

Corporate Culture and Local Culture

In the workplace these days, we often have to work with people from different cultural backgrounds. When a multinational company sets up a branch abroad, it might soon find its corporate culture sometimes conflicts with the local culture.

For example, most American companies have egalitarian management styles, but when they move to China, they find that hierarchy is highly valued there. In Japan, a seniority system has been the tradition, which usually means promotion is based on the length of working years in a company. Of course, such a practice clashes with the American basis of promotion, namely, employees' performances. In Southeast Asia and Latin America, group harmony is often so emphasized that any open confrontation has to be avoided. In many western companies, employees are encouraged to debate openly and to brainstorm together. It is generally believed that this attribute of open corporate culture is a key driving force in many innovative tech-companies.

As a final point, it is up to the managing teams to decide to what extent they want to adapt to the local culture and how to nurture the right kind of international corporate culture for themselves.

企業文化與當地文化

現今的職場上經常會遇到必須與不同文化背景的人共事的機會，當跨國公司在海外設立分公司時，很快就會發生企業文化與當地文化衝突的現象。

例如，大部分美國企業的管理風格為人人平等，但是到了中國馬上就會發現當地盛行等級制度；在日本，傳統上實行年資制度，這意味著升遷是以在公司服務時間的長短作為依據，當然這樣的作法與美國依表現來決定升遷的制度相衝突。在東南亞與拉丁美洲，經常過度強調團體的和諧，以至於任何的公開衝突都要避免；而很多西方企業鼓勵員工公開辯論，一起腦力激盪，一般認為，這樣的企業文化特質是很多創新的科技公司能進步的關鍵趨動力。

最後要強調的一點是，一切還是要由管理團隊來決定要如何適應當地文化，還有如何培養出適合自己類型的國際企業文化。

字彙與片語

* egalitarian [ɪ͵gælɪ'tɛrɪən] a. 平等主義的
* hierarchy ['haɪə͵rɑrkɪ] n. 等級制度
* seniority [sin'jɔrətɪ] n. 老資格的特權；年長；年資
* confrontation [͵kɑnfrʌn'teʃən] n. 對抗
* nurture ['nɝtʃɚ] v. 培養

3. Terminology 財經專業術語

corporate culture　企業文化

是指一個企業由其共有的價值觀、處事方式、信念等內化認同而表現出的特有行為模式，從中可以觀察到組織人員的行為規律、工作的團體規範、組織信奉的主要價值等等。

seniority system　年資系統

公司員工的升遷與福利是依據年紀和資歷而定，而不是只有靠工作表現來決定。

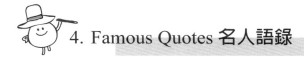

4. Famous Quotes 名人語錄

Corporate culture matters. How management chooses to treat its people impacts everything — for better or for worse.

Simon Sinek

企業文化非常重要，管理階層如何選擇對待員工的方式對一切的影響都非常大──不論是好的或壞的影響。

賽門・席內克

A sour corporate culture can actually make an entire society unhappy. This means that a strong corporate culture can have a positive impact on a society.

Simon Sinek

一個腐敗的企業文化會令整個社會感到不幸，這也代表了一個健全的企業文化能對社會產生正面的影響。

賽門・席內克

In corporate culture, in sports culture, in the media, we honor those who win at all costs.

Jackson Katz

無論在企業文化、運動文化、媒體，人們都讚許那些不惜一切手段只求獲勝的人。

傑克森・卡茲

It all sounds almost silly, but the fact is that the only way to change a corporate culture is to just change it.

Gordon Bethune

聽起來有點笨，不過事實上，改變企業文化的唯一方法就是去做改變。

高爾登・貝修恩

Samsung's future hinges on new businesses, new products and new technologies. We should make our corporate culture more open, flexible and innovative.

Lee Kun-hee

三星集團的未來取決於新產業、新產品、新科技，我們應該讓企業文化變得更開放，更有彈性，更創新。

李健熙

1. Dialogue 實境對話　4-3

A: Some of your subordinates have problems with your leadership.

B: Are they implying that I do not have what it takes to be a good leader?

A: Not exactly.

B: Does it have something to do with the way I look?

A: Your appearance is quite all right, but there seems to be some issues with the way you act.

B: Can you be a bit more specific than that?

A: For example, when dealing with a crisis, you are not calm and decisive enough.

B: How can you tell?

A: In the ways you communicate with your subordinates.

B: How do I sound to you?

A: Pretty lacking in confidence, I would say. People around you can just feel it.

B: It probably has much to do with the tones I use. I simply don't like to boss people around.

A: You do not have to sound bossy or aggressive, but you do have to be assertive.

B: I see what you mean. Thank you for pointing out my weaknesses, so I can work on them.

中文翻譯

A：你的下屬中有些人對你領導人的方式有意見。

B：他們是在暗指我沒有帶人的本領嗎？

A：也不盡然。

B：是我看起來的樣子有問題嗎？

A：你的外表沒問題，但是你的行事風格似乎有點問題。

B：你能不能說得再仔細點？

A：例如，處理危機時你不夠冷靜，不夠果決。

B：你怎麼知道的呢？

A：由你和下屬溝通的方式得知。

B：你感覺我聽起來怎麼樣？

A：我覺得很沒有自信，在你周圍的人就是可以感覺到。

B：這可能和我所使用的語氣有很大的關係，我就是不喜歡對人頤指氣使。

A：你不需要對人頤指氣使或口氣很衝，但是你必須要態度堅定。

B：我明白你的意思了，謝謝你指出我的弱點，好讓我改進。

- subordinate [sə'bɔrdnɪt] n. 部下，部屬

- specific [spɪ'sɪfɪk] a. 明確的；具體的；特定的

- bossy ['bɑsɪ] a. 愛指揮他人的，跋扈的

- aggressive [ə'grɛsɪv] a. 好鬥的，挑釁的；侵略的

- assertive [ə'sɝtɪv] a. 肯定的，堅定自信的

Leadership

A great leader should act ethically in all situations. Integrity is reflected in the leader's decision-making, and integrity is the fundamental core of the image the company is building. Everything in an enterprise evolves naturally from the ethics of leadership.

In this complicated world we are living in, almost all issues involve the stakeholders of different interests. An excellent leader must be able to act efficiently. That's why we need a leader to negotiate and to handle crises. This requires great communication skills. Expressing a complex thing in a simple way is not an easy task, and explaining it in a clear way that all people can accept is even more challenging. A capable leader should be able to master the art of communication.

Charisma is often one of the attributes people speak of when they talk about leadership. It is based on the confidence of being a true leader, able to direct and delegate the issues of the company. To sum up, being ethical, having strong communication skills and being charismatic are qualities of an outstanding leader.

本文翻譯

領導力

一個優秀領導人的行為必須要能在任何情形下都合乎道德，誠信反映在一個領導人的決策過程，是公司正在建立的形象的基礎核心，公司內的所有事情都會隨著領導的道德而自然發展。

在我們所處的這個複雜世界中，幾乎所有的事情都會牽涉到不同利益的利害關係人，一個優秀的領導者必須要能有效行動，這就是為什麼我們需要領導人來協調與處理危機，需要非常良好的溝通技巧。能將複雜的事情用簡單的方式來表達並不容易，如果要用清楚明白的方式讓所有人都能接受更是具有挑戰性，一個有能力的領導者必須完全掌握溝通的藝術。

領袖魅力常被人們視作是領導力的特質之一，它的基礎在於身為真正領導人的信心，相信擁有督導和分派公司事項之能力。總而言之，有道德且有良好的溝通能力，並有領袖魅力，可以說是一位傑出領導者所不可或缺的特質。

字彙與片語

- ethically [ˈɛθɪklɪ] adv. 有道德地；道德上
- integrity [ɪnˈtɛɡrətɪ] n. 正直；廉正；誠實
- fundamental [ˌfʌndəˈmɛnt!] a. 基礎的；根本的，十分重要的
- stakeholder [ˈstekˌholdɚ] n. 利害關係人
- charisma [kəˈrɪzmə] n. 非凡的領導力；魅力

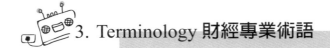# 3. Terminology 財經專業術語

leadership　領導力

　　關於領導力的定義很多，有人認為，領導者是處於組織變化和活動的核心地位，並努力實現願景的人；也有人認為，領導力是一個人先天具有的，能夠引導他人完成任務的特點和性格合成的；還有人認為，領導力與領導者及其下屬之間的權力關係有關，領導者具有權力來影響他人；還有，領導力是一種達成目標的工具，協助團體內部成員實現其目標。

team management　團隊管理

　　團隊管理是指在一個組織中，依成員工作性質、能力組成各種小組，參與組織各項決定和解決問題等事務，以提高組織生產力並且達成組織目標。

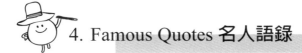# 4. Famous Quotes 名人語錄

Innovation distinguishes between a leader and a follower.

Steve Jobs

創新是領導人與追隨者的差別所在。

史蒂夫・賈柏斯

If your actions inspire others to dream more, learn more, do more and become more, you are a leader.

John Quincy Adams

如果你的行為可以啓發他人有更多的夢想，進行更多的學習，去做更多的事，成爲更有成就的人，你就是位領導人。

約翰 · 昆西 · 亞當斯

. . . .

Leadership is the capacity to translate vision into reality.

Warren Bennis

領導力就是能將願景轉變爲事實的能力。

瓦倫 · 班尼斯

. . . .

I am not afraid of an army of lions led by a sheep; I am afraid of an army of sheep led by a lion.

Alexander the Great

我不擔心一群獅子所組成的軍隊，由一隻綿羊來當領導者；我擔心的是一群綿羊由一隻獅子來領導。

亞力山大大帝

. . . .

Leadership and learning are indispensable to each other.

John F. Kennedy

領導力與學習兩者為互補關係，缺一不可。

約翰・甘迺迪

Communication
溝通

1. Dialogue 實境對話 4-4

A: You look very frustrated. What happened?

B: It's about the work I've had to do this February. Our manager gave lots of assignments to me again. My colleague seems to get away with a smaller workload because he said he was going to take his family abroad during the Chinese New Year holiday.

A: Have you tried to talk with your manager about it?

B: No, I am not going anywhere during the holidays. Besides, I'm worried I would come across as difficult if I complain too much.

A: You should step up in a situation like this.

B: Last time, when I talked about this issue with our manager, he simply said he gave me more work because I was more capable than others.

A: Did he give you some recognition, or reward you in any way?

B: Just some verbal compliments.

A: If you feel that your workload is unfairly heavy, you should have a candid talk with your manager. If he is a sensible boss, he will do something about it.

B: Let's hope so.

中文翻譯

A： 你看起來很沮喪，發生了什麼事情？

B： 是關於二月份我必須要做的工作，我們經理又給了我很多工作，而我的同事似乎可以做較少的工作，因為他說在農曆春節要帶他家人出國玩。

A： 你是否和你們經理談過了呢？

B： 沒有，我在春節期間沒有要上哪兒去，除此之外，我擔心如果我一直抱怨，會顯得我難相處。

A： 在這種情形下，你應該要站出來說話。

B： 上次我和我們經理談這個問題時，他只是說他給我較多的工作是因為我的能力比別人強。

A： 他會給你什麼認可或獎勵嗎？

B： 只是口頭上的讚美。

A： 要是你覺得工作量太重且不公平，就應該要與你們經理坦率談談，如果你的老闆是明理人，他就會處理這件事。

B： 希望如此。

- come across 被理解爲
- recognition [ˌrɛkəg'nɪʃən] n. 賞識；表彰；報償
- verbal ['vɝb!] a. 言辭上的；言語的，字句的
- compliment ['kɑmpləmənt] n. 讚美的話；恭維；敬意
- sensible ['sɛnsəb!] a. 明智的；合情理的

2. Article 文章

How to Communicate Effectively

The key point in communicating with others is to believe that there is an end goal to accomplish in the process of negotiation. If you do not think there is a possible solution, then you have programmed yourself for failure in the end. Without trying all possible means to reach an agreement with the other party, you can never say that you have done your best to improve the current situation.

This does not mean that you do not have to assess all the risks involved in communicating and simply insist on going ahead with the negotiation. Putting yourself in the shoes of others can often change your perspective of things. For example, maybe you feel that you have contributed quite a lot to your company, and you ask for a raise that you think is overdue. Your boss might think that the company is not doing very well financially and you should have known it. If you do not care about anything else and ask for a raise, the likelihood for you to get the raise would probably be very little. Of course, making sense of the timing is not always easy, but generally speaking, it comes naturally with work experience.

The way you communicate plays an important role, too. Nobody likes to feel threatened by others, so make an effort to control the tone of your voice. Being dominant is not always a good way of addressing others; yet being too humble might make people feel that you are not very firm with your position. If you can make the other party feel you are genuine and sincere, your chance of getting success in your communication is often quite high.

本文翻譯

如何有效溝通

　　與他人溝通最關鍵的是要能在協商的過程中相信溝通過程可以達成某個目標，如果你不相信可能會有解決方法，那麼你已經為自己設定好了最後會失敗。如果沒有試過所有可能方式來與對方和解，就不能說你已經盡了力去改善現況。

　　這並不代表你不需衡量溝通中會牽涉到的所有風險，一昧堅持談判下去。站在對方的立場去思考常可以改變你看事情的角度，例如，或許你覺得你對公司貢獻相當大，於是你要求加薪，而且相信早就該加薪了，但是你的老闆可能認為公司現在獲利不多，這點你該知道，如果你什麼都不管就要求加薪，那麼你能獲得加薪的可能性就非常低。當然，掌握時機不總是那麼容易，但是一般來說，隨著工作經驗的增多也就越來越容易。

　　你溝通的方式也很重要，沒有人喜歡被別人威脅，所以努力控制好你說話的語調，強勢並非總是對他人說話的好方法，但是太過謙卑會讓人覺得你對自己立場不是很堅定，如果你能讓對方感到很真心誠懇，你溝通能成功的機率就相當高了。

字彙與片語

● assess [ə'sɛs] v. 估算，評價

- risk [rɪsk] n. 危險，風險
- overdue ['ovɚ'dju] a. 過期的
- threaten ['θrɛtn]] v. 威脅
- dominant ['dɑmənənt] a. 強勢的

3. Terminology 財經專業術語

communication　溝通

　　所謂溝通，是人與人之間的思想和訊息的交換，是將訊息由一個人傳達給另一個人，逐漸廣泛傳播的過程。著名組織管理學家巴納德認為，溝通是把一個組織中的成員聯繫在一起，以實現共同目標的手段，沒有溝通，就沒有管理。溝通不良幾乎是每個企業都存在的老毛病，企業的機構越是複雜，其溝通越是困難，往往基層的許多建設性意見還未回饋至高層決策者，便已被層層扼殺，而高層決策的傳達，常常也無法以原貌展現在所有人員之前。

communication management　溝通管理

　　溝通管理是創造和提升企業精神和企業文化，完成企業管理根本目標的主要方式和工具。管理的最高境界就是在企業經營管理中創造出一種企業獨有的企業精神和企業文化，使企業管理的外在需求轉化為企業員工內在的觀念和自覺的行為模式，認同企業核心的價值觀念和目標及使命。而企業精神與企業文化的培育與塑造，其實質是一種思想、觀點、情感的溝通，是管理溝通的最高形式和內容，沒有溝通，

就沒有對企業精神和企業文化的理解與共識，更不可能認同企業共同使命。

 communication capability　溝通能力

　　一般說來，溝通能力是指溝通者所具備的能勝任溝通工作的優良主觀條件；簡言之，人際溝通的能力指一個人與他人有效地進行溝通訊息的能力，包括溝通技巧和人個特質。

4. Famous Quotes 名人語錄

Wise men speak because they have something to say; fools because they have to say something.

Plato

智者說話是因為他們有話要說；愚者說話則是因為他們必須得要說些什麼。

柏拉圖

....

The most important thing in communication is hearing what isn't said.

Peter Drucker

溝通最重要的就是要聽出沒有說出的意思。

彼得 · 杜魯克

I do not agree with what you have to say, but I'll defend to the death your right to say it.

Voltaire

我不同意你所說的話，不過我至死都會捍衛你有說這話的權利。

伏爾太

. . . .

Of all of our inventions for mass communication, pictures still speak the most universally understood language.

Walt Disney

在所有大眾傳播的發明中，圖像仍是世上到處最容易爲所有人明白的語言。

華特・迪斯耐

. . . .

Brevity is the soul of wit.

William Shakespeare

簡潔是機智的靈魂。

威廉・莎士比亞

Unit 5 Negotiation 談判

1. Dialogue 實境對話 🎧 4-5

A: May I hold an exhibition of my paintings in your gallery?

B: Of course. As you know, our gallery is in Chung-Li and it is hard to attract famous artists.

A: I went to senior high school in Chung-Li, and it's good to be back. This is a catalog of my last exhibition. This time I would like to show my oil paintings.

B: From this catalog, I can see you incorporated many Taiwanese elements in your artwork.

A: After returning from France to Taiwan, I found myself paying more attention to our own unique items than before.

B: I particularly like this series of the Lunar New Year's celebration.

A: If so, I can give this set of the paintings of fireworks to you.

B: Thank you very much. What can I do in return for your exhibition in the gallery?

A: Is it possible for me to use the showing space from June 1 to August 31 this year?

B: Would you be willing to host an open evening on the first day of the exhibition?

A: Sure. In fact, I'm thinking about giving the visitors free tours myself.

B: That's very nice of you. It's our pleasure to host your artwork.

中文翻譯

A： 我可以在您的畫廊舉辦畫展嗎？

B： 當然，您也知道，我們的畫廊位於中壢，很難吸引有名的藝術家過來。

A： 我曾在中壢唸高中，能回來真好，這是我上次畫展的目錄，這次我想要展示我的油畫。

B： 從目錄可以看出您將很多台灣的元素納入作品中。

A： 自從法國回到台灣後，我發現自己比從前更加注意我們獨有的事物。

B： 我特別喜歡這一系列的農曆新年慶祝活動。

A： 這樣子的話，我可以給您這一組煙火畫。

B： 非常感謝，我能為您在我們畫廊即將舉辦的畫展做些什麼來回報呢？

A： 請問我可以在今年6月1日到8月31日使用展覽空間嗎？

B： 您願意在展覽首日傍晚舉行開幕式嗎？

A： 當然好，事實上，我想要親自為參觀者做免費導覽。

B： 您真好心，展示您的藝術作品是我們的榮幸。

- negotiation [nɪ,goʃɪ'eʃən] n. 談判，協商
- catalog ['kætəlɔg] n. 目錄
- incorporate [ɪn'kɔrpə,ret] v. 吸收；併入
- artwork ['ɑrt,wɝk] n. 美術品；藝術品
- unique [ju'nik] a. 獨一無二的；獨特的

Negotiation

In the world of business, negotiation skills are absolutely essential. If we try to talk to the best part of the other person sincerely, we can largely reduce the time it takes to achieve an agreement. The final result of the negotiation will suit both parties as well.

Do your homework and find out the bargaining chips, which can give you a competitive edge in negotiation. Before the negotiation, keep in mind the possible criteria and move towards optimizing the conditions. This requires thorough researching beforehand and attentive listening in the process of the negotiation. Avoid personal attacks and remain composed when the other party seems to lose its temper. It is the words that count most in a conversation, but the tone and voice volume also carry meaningful messages. Sometimes words unsaid are even more important than words said.

We've all heard that we should put ourselves in the other's shoes. This does not mean we should think for the other person to the point of ignoring our needs. In fact, considering their perspective helps us most. It serves our interests to know what their intentions are. Most importantly, this helps us to access the chances for reaching an agreement between them and us. It would be ideal if the agreement could satisfy both parties. Nevertheless, we should note that it is not necessarily a failure to walk out of the situation in order to protect our best interests in the end.

本文翻譯

談判

在商場上，談判技巧非常重要，如果我們試著誠懇地與對方最好的一面交談，我們可以大幅減少為了要達成和解所需的時間，談判最後的結果會對彼此都很合宜。

做足功課，找出談判籌碼，這樣可以在協商中為你帶來競爭優勢，在談判前要記住所有可能的基本要求，然後盡力改善情況，這需要事先周詳的研究，並且在協商過程中專心聆聽。避免人身攻擊，而且要在對方似乎快失去理智時保持冷靜。在交談中最重要的是用詞，但是，所用的語調與音量也同樣富有意義，有時候，沒有說出的話比說出的話還來得重要。

我們都聽過要站立在對方的角度去思考，這並不表示我們應該為對方想，到了忽略我們自身需要的程度。事實上，考慮對方立場對我們的幫助最大，了解別人的目的對我們助益良多，最重要的，這幫助我們達成與對方的和解。最後的和解如果能讓雙方滿意固然很理想，但是我們該謹記，如果最後為了保護自己權益而放棄談判，也並不一定就算是一場失敗。

字彙與片語

- bargaining chip 談判籌碼
- competitive [kəm'pɛtətɪv] a. 競爭的
- edge [ɛdʒ] n. 優勢，優越條件
- criterion [kraɪ'tɪrɪən] n. 判斷的標準（複數為 criteria）
- optimize ['ɑptə,maɪz] v. 充分利用；使……最優化
- composed [kəm'pozd] a. 鎮靜的；沉著的

3. Terminology 財經專業術語

negotiation　談判

談判有廣義與狹義之分：廣義的談判是指除正式場合下的談判外，一切協商、交涉、商量、磋商等等，都可以視為談判；狹義的談判僅僅是指正式場合下的談判。

sales negotiation　銷售談判

銷售談判是工商談判中最主要的類型，也是本書討論的重點。在銷售談判中，賣主關心的是賣價的高低和銷售量的多少，買主關心的是產品的質量和服務的各項條件以及價格上的優惠。談判的主要內容包括總價、質量要求、特殊服務、包裝、運輸、付費方式、交貨時間、出貨時間等等。

🍺bargaining chips 談判籌碼

談判籌碼是談判時對自己有利的條件或情勢。籌碼（chip）為賭博或遊戲中用來代替錢幣的器具，此有將籌碼兌換成現金之意，握有越多籌碼，則越有贏得談判的勝算，可獲得越多的利益。

 4. Famous Quotes 名人語錄

Negotiation means getting the best of your opponent.

Marvin Gaye

協商的意義是要引出你的對手心中最善良之處。

馬爾文・蓋耶

....

Everything is negotiable. Whether or not the negotiation is easy is another thing.

Carrie Fisher

每件事都是可以協商的，只不過協商是否容易又是另一回事了。

凱利・費雪

....

So much of life is a negotiation — so even if you're not in business, you have opportunities to practice all around you.

Kevin O'Leary

人生有很大一部分都在談判——即使你不從商，仍然有很多機會可以在周遭練習談判。

凱文 · 毆黎理

....

The most difficult thing in any negotiation, almost, is making sure that you strip it of the emotion and deal with the facts. And there was a considerable challenge to that here and understandably so.

Howard Baker

任何談判中最困難的便是要完全不帶感情地去處理事實，而要做到如此是很大的挑戰，理由是很顯而易見的。

霍華德 · 貝克

....

If you're a politician, you might want to learn the Buddhist way of negotiation. Restoring communication and bringing back reconciliation is clear and concrete in Buddhism.

Thich Nhat Hanh

如果你是從政者，或許你會想學習佛教談判的方式，在佛教教義中，恢復溝通與達成和解是很清楚明確的。

一行禪師

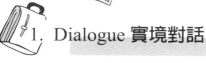

Unit 6 Discrimination in the Workplace
職場上的歧視

1. Dialogue 實境對話 4-6

Jessica: Could you please tell me why I was not promoted to the manager position?

Boss: Based on the general evaluations last year, Kevin is more qualified than you to be promoted to the manager position.

Jessica: Please take a close look at my work performance so far. What made you think that I was less capable than Kevin to get the promotion?

Boss: The decision was the result of a vote by the board of directors.

Jessica: And all of the members are male.

Boss: What are you trying to imply?

Jessica: Maybe this is gender discrimination? Maybe this company is just not ready for a female manager yet?

Boss: This allegation is baseless.

Jessica: Do you really think I am not good enough to be promoted to be a manager?

Boss: In my opinion, your capabilities are certainly good, but Kevin happens to have more work experience than you.

Jessica: I guess you are right. Perhaps I should work with him for a while to gain more experience.

Boss: You can learn a lot from him, especially his leadership skills.

中文翻譯

潔西卡：你可不可以告訴我，為什麼我不能被升為經理？

老　闆：從去年的總評量看來，凱文比你還有資格被升為經理。

潔西卡：請仔細看我至今的工作表現，到底哪一點讓你認為我比他沒有資格被升為經理？

老　闆：這是董事會投票決定的。

潔西卡：所有的董事成員都是男性。

老　闆：你在暗示什麼呢？

潔西卡：或許這是性別歧視？或許這家公司就是還沒準備好有個女性當經理？

老　闆：這樣的指控毫無根據。

潔西卡：你真的認為我的能力還不夠好到能被升為經理？

老　闆：依我看來，你的能力當然是很強，但是凱文剛好有較多的工作經驗。

潔西卡：我猜你說的對，或許我需要和他一起工作一陣子，以獲得更多的經驗。

老　闆：你可以從他身上學到很多東西，特別是他的領導能力。

- discrimination [dɪ͵skrɪmə'neʃən] n. 不公平待遇，歧視

- evaluation [ɪ͵væljʊ'eʃən] n. 評價

- gender ['dʒɛndɚ] n. 性別

- allegation [͵ælə'geʃən] n. 指責；指控

- baseless ['beslɪs] a. 無根據的，無理由的

Discrimination in the Workplace

Discrimination exists almost everywhere, including the workplace. With an unbalanced power system, people involved can probably get very frustrated, not knowing what to do about it. The following three types of discrimination are most frequently seen among employers and employees: gender discrimination, age discrimination and racial discrimination. When it is the combination of more than one type, the situation can become very complicated.

Although most companies claim that gender discrimination does not exist in their workplace, many women feel the "glass ceiling" effect as soon as they reach certain executive levels. This is a barrier almost all female employees can feel but find it hard to break through. Some employers say they would hire more women for the top positions if the female applicants were as good as the males. What they don't want to admit is that the hiring process is so biased that a quota system for females has to be introduced. Usually, being young is considered an asset when applying for a job, but increasingly, many companies value solid, related working experiences, which senior applicants are more likely to have. With the prolonged average life expectancy, flexibility with age in hiring has become the trend. Quite a few people do have some rooted prejudices against certain races. Racial discrimination is hard to fight against because it is often quite subtle and difficult to avoid completely.

The direct victims of discrimination might be hurt, but their colleagues around them might not have the slightest idea of what's going on in the office. As time goes by, more people may start to be affected, but they might have already missed the best time to deal with the discrimination. That's why we need courageous ones to gather evidence and step up, and we also need the Human Resources department to handle it effectively.

本文翻譯

職場上的歧視

歧視幾乎無所不在，職場也不例外，在權力系統不平衡的時候，相關人士可能會感到非常沮喪，不知道該如何處理。接下來的歧視是雇主與員工之間最常見的三種歧視：性別歧視、年紀歧視、種族歧視，如果是其中多於一種的合併，情況可以變得非常複雜。

雖然大部分公司都宣稱他們職場上沒有性別歧視，但是很多做到某種主管階級的女性都感覺到一種玻璃效應。這是一種障礙，大多女性員工都可以感受得到，但是卻難以突破。有些雇主說只要女性求職者和男性一樣好，他們就會雇用女性來擔任高階職位，但是他們不願意承認的是，錄用人才的過程是如此充滿偏見，以至於必須要使用定額分配制。通常年紀輕會被視為求職時的一項資產，但是越來越多公司重視豐富的相關經驗，而年紀大的求職者的工作經驗通常較多。現在平均壽命普遍延長，對年紀的要求變得有彈性，已經是招募人才的趨勢。有不少人對某些種族有著根深柢固的偏見，種族偏見很難去除，因為常是非常微妙且難以完全避免。

　　歧視的直接受害者可能受到傷害，但是他們周圍的同事可能完全不知道辦公室發生了什麼事。隨著時間過去，更多的人可能會開始受到影響，不過他們可能已經錯過處理歧視的最佳時機。這就是為什麼我們需要有勇氣的人來搜集資料，挺身而出，也需要人事部門來有效處理相關事項。

字彙與片語

- barrier ['bærɪr] n. 障礙，阻礙
- biased ['baɪəst] a. 存有偏見的；偏見的
- quota ['kwotə] n. 配額；定額；限額
- asset ['æsɛt] n. 資產
- prolonged [prə'lɔŋd] a. 延長的
- subtle ['sʌt!] a. 微妙的，隱約的

3. Terminology 財經專業術語

discrimination in the workplace　職場歧視

　　職場歧視是指在工作場所中，某種類型的勞動力群體不願意與另外一種勞動力群體相互合作或共事，發生例如性別、性向、年紀、種族的不平等待遇。

reverse discrimination　逆向歧視

所謂逆向歧視是指為追求實質平等，對特定群體或個人給予的特定保護超過了必要的限度，而形成的對一般群體或個人的不合理差別對待或制度安排，其表現形式為對特定群體的過度保護、照顧和特別優惠措施。

4. Famous Quotes 名人語錄

Obama signed the Lilly Ledbetter Fair Pay Act to ensure fair pay for women in the workplace. In addition, he succeeded in getting a measure passed to end discrimination against gays in the military.

Kitty Kelley

歐巴馬總統簽下了莉莉雷德貝特平等薪資法案，好讓婦女在工作場所得到平等的薪水。除此之外，歐巴馬也成功推動了終止軍隊中歧視同性戀者的措施。

凱特・凱利

We cannot ensure that women will be free of discrimination in the workplace and everywhere as long as women are not universally defended under our Constitution. As it stands now, the equal rights of women are subject to interpretation of law. That is a risk our mothers, sisters and daughters cannot afford.

Carolyn Maloney

如果婦女沒有完全受到我們憲法的保護，我們就不能保證婦女在工作場所或其它地方不會受到歧視。就現況看來，婦女平權議題全看對法條的解釋而定，這可是我們的母親、姊妹、女兒們所無法承受的風險。

卡羅琳 · 馬羅尼

....

The saddest part of the human race is we're obsessed with this idea of 'us and them,' which is really a no-win situation, whether it's racial, cultural, religious or political.

Dave Matthews

人們最令人感到難過的一點就是，總是在想著「我們、你們」這個問題，沒有人真能從這樣的局勢中獲得好處，無論是在種族、文化、宗教、政治上都是如此。

戴夫 · 馬修

....

We must stand for the right of every American to practice their faith according to the dictates of their conscience, whether it be in the public square or in the workplace.

Mike Pence

我們必須堅定支持每個美國人都有依其良心從事宗教活動的權利，無論是在公共廣場或工作場所都是如此。

麥克 · 龐斯

Unit 7　Public Relations
公共關係

1. Dialogue 實境對話　4-7

A: This Saturday there is a public tree planting campaign in the neighborhood. I think we should take part in the activity.

B: What good can this community work do for us?

A: We are in the energy business, which is highly related to environmental protection. If we join the activity, it will be very good for our public image and also boost our public relations.

B: Will there be media coverage there?

A: Of course. On that day, all school kids in this neighborhood are encouraged by their teachers to plant trees in the small farms nearby. Government reporters and newspaper journalists will be there for sure.

B: Should we set up stands and give out small free gifts?

A: I'm thinking about giving some sunflower seeds for participants to plant.

B: In that case, we should talk with the farmers about arranging the farm land to grow sunflowers.

A: They would be very delighted to hear about this plan.

B: I'll let you take care of this event and don't forget to ask our photographers to take photos during this campaign as well.

A：這星期六這個社區有個公開的植樹宣傳活動，我認為我們應該參加。

B：這個社區活動對我們有什麼好處呢？

A：我們是做能源產業的，與環境保護息息相關，如果我們參加這個活動，非常有益於我們的公開形象，也會使我們的公共關係大大加分。

B：會有媒體到那兒採訪嗎？

A：當然，當天老師會鼓勵所有的學童在附近的農場種樹，官方記者與報紙新聞記者一定都會到那兒。

B：我們應該設立攤位，分發免費小贈品嗎？

A：我正在考慮給參與者向日葵種子來播種。

B：那麼我該與農友討論安排農地以供種植向日葵。

A：他們如果知道了這個計劃，一定會很高興。

B：我就讓你來處理這個活動，不要忘了也請我們的攝影師於這個活動中照相。

字彙與片語

- relate [rɪˈlet] v. 有關，涉及
- boost [bust] v. 推動；幫助；促進
- coverage [ˈkʌvərɪdʒ] n. 新聞報導

- participant [pɑrˈtɪsəpənt] n. 參與者
- delight [dɪˈlaɪt] v. 使高興

2. Article 文章

Public Relations

When people talk about public relations, they generally mean using public media, such as trade presses, to promote their companies. In contrast to advertising and marketing, companies do not have to pay for public relations. Thus the credibility of objective media, such as a mainstream newspaper, carries much more weight than paid advertisements. The effects of a public relations campaign also last much longer than those of a marketing event.

The most important point in public relations is to get your professional expertise publicly recognized by the target market. Of course, in the beginning, this involves doing voluntary service to get exposure for your company, or submitting one or two of your articles to the trade magazines run by your union. Depending on the business you are in, there are various tactics you can employ to make your name known via public activities. Assess the results of these efforts every few months, and you will know how flexible you should be when approaching similar issues.

One thing to keep in mind is that in order to stand out among many competitors, you have to be really able to offer what you promise your customers. Public relations are only tools to make the market customers know of your existence, but they cannot enhance the quality of your products or services at all.

本文翻譯

公共關係

當人們談論公共關係時，通常指的是使用公共媒體，例如業界刊物來宣傳企業。相對於廣告和行銷，公司不需要為公共關係付費，因此客觀的媒體會比付費的廣告有更大的說服力，例如主流的報紙，公共關係的活動所產生的效果也比行銷活動來得深遠。

公共關係最重要的一點是使得你的專業技術為目標市場公開承認。當然，在剛開始時，這牽涉到需要提供義務服務來獲得公司的曝光度，或是向你的工會經營的專業雜誌提供一兩篇你寫的文章。依照你的產業之不同而有各種的方式，透過公開活動來增加你的知名度。每隔幾個月評估努力的結果，就會知道遇到類似議題時該要有多大的彈性。

要謹記在心的是，為了要在眾多競爭者中脫穎而出，你必須真能兌現你對顧客的承諾，公共關係只是讓目標顧客知道你存在的手段，但是卻一點也不能提高你的產品或服務的品質。

- press [prɛs] n. 報刊

- credibility [ˌkrɛdə'bɪlətɪ] n. 可信性;確實性

- objective [əb'dʒɛktɪv] a. 客觀的

- tactics ['tæktɪks] n. 策略,手段

- enhance [ɪn'hæns] v. 提高,增加

3. Terminology 財經專業術語

public relations　公共關係

公共關係主要從事組織機構的訊息傳播，協調對外的關係，處理組織或公司的形象管理事項。

public relations activity　公關活動

公關活動是指一個組織為創造良好的社會環境，爭取公眾輿論支持而採取的政策和行動，主要是透過傳播溝通與協調等手段，以創造良好的公共關係為目的的一種訊息溝通活動。

public relation practitioner (PR Practitioner)　公關人員

公關人員指的是從事公共關係工作的人員，作為一名專業的公關從業人員，首先應具備合理的專業知識與技能，其次應有較強的綜合與溝通能力，此外還必須有良好的道德品格。

4. Famous Quotes 名人語錄

I'm not doing my philanthropic work, out of any kind of guilt, or any need to create good public relations. I'm doing it because I can afford to do it, and I believe in it.

George Soros

我從事慈善事業並非因爲任何的罪惡感，或是爲了營造任何良好的公共關係，而是因爲我負擔得起，而且我相信這樣做有意義。

喬治 · 索羅斯

Parliamentarians certainly know how to do bad public relations.

Heather Brooke

那些擅長辯論的國會議員眞是會製造惡質的公共關係。

海勒 · 布魯克

I've gotten more press than any entrepreneur could dream of — certainly more than I deserve — and I've never had a public relations firm working for me.

Jason Calacanis

我所得到的媒體報導遠比其他的創業家都來得多——顯然比我值得的報導多很多——而且我從來沒有雇用過一家公關公司爲我工作過。

傑森 · 卡拉卡尼斯

Some are born great, some achieve greatness, and some hire public relations officers.

Daniel Boorstin

有些人生來就很偉大，有些人成就非凡，還有另一些人就光靠雇用公關人員來做宣傳。

丹尼爾・布爾斯汀

Chapter 5   Innovation

創新

Unit 1　Sharing Economy
共享經濟

1. Dialogue 實境對話　　5-1

A: I just took Uber to come here.

B: Haven't you heard the many negative reports about Uber?

A: Most news reports are negative anyway. So far I've never had any bad experiences with Uber.

B: I heard that many Uber drivers are not certified, and there is almost no insurance whatsoever.

A: In my experience, they seem to be very professional and efficient.

B: Have you given your personal contact details to them?

A: Yes, I had to, otherwise, how could I let them know when and where to pick me up?

B: Aren't you afraid they will document your personal data for business use?

A: But with a traditional taxi service, it is quite similar. I always make a phone call when I need a taxi.

B: Except that Uber drivers are equipped with smarter devices to track your routines, where your office and home are located, etc.

A: I can't see why they would be that interested in my personal data.

B: First, it's useful for Uber to study their customers, and then they can sell the valuable information to other businesses for commercial purposes.

A: Don't they have some kind of privacy policies?

B: Uber is notorious for their infamous corporate culture.

A: Hopefully, they would not reveal my whereabouts to others.

中文翻譯

A： 我剛搭Uber來這裡。

B： 你沒有聽說不少關於Uber的負面報導嗎？

A： 大部分新聞報導總是很負面，至今我還沒有任何搭Uber的不良經驗。

B： 我聽說很多Uber的司機都沒有司機證件，而且根本沒有任何的保險。

A： 在我的經驗裡，他們似乎都很專業，很有效率。

B： 你是否曾將你的個人連絡方式給他們？

A： 我必須要給他們，不然我怎麼讓他們知道何時何地來載我？

B： 你難道不怕他們會將你的個人資料的紀錄用於商業用途嗎？

A： 但是傳統的計程車服務也很相似，我需要計程車時都會打電話叫車。

B： 不過Uber駕駛可是有更精明的配備，可以紀錄行車路徑，還有你的辦公室與住家的所在處等等。

A：我看不出他們為什麼會對我的個人資料那麼有興趣。

B：第一，Uber會想研究他們的客人，這對他們很有用，再者他們可以將這些資料為了商業目的，賣給其它公司。

A：他們難道沒有什麼隱私權政策嗎？

B：Uber可是因為劣質的企業文化而惡名昭彰。

A：希望他們不會將我的行蹤洩露出去。

字彙與片語

- negative ['nɛgətɪv] a. 負面的，反面的
- routine [ru'tin] n. 例行公事；日常工作
- commercial [kə'mɝʃəl] a. 商業的；商務的
- notorious [no'torɪəs] a. 惡名昭彰的，聲名狼藉的
- infamous ['ɪnfəməs] a. 聲名狼藉的，臭名昭著的

Sharing Economy

A sharing economy is also called a collaborative economy, and it is often based on social media or other mobile information technology. The idea is that a member of a social community provides goods or services to another at little or no costs. In this way, precious resources are sufficiently used and not wasted. Many people who practice a sharing economy believe that it is indeed a game-changer.

One typical example is Airbnb, which is a platform for people to list, find, and rent spaces for accommodation. Through Airbnb, many backpackers have found rooms quickly and easily. Quite a lot of elderly couples provide Airbnb with empty rooms left by their children. Both hosts and guests are encouraged to write their comments about each other in their profiles for new members to view. So far, there have been many good reports from the hosts and guests, but there have also been some ill-intentioned people who abuse this platform.

Hotel owners find Airbnb extremely disruptive, and they criticize Airbnb for not abiding by hotel business regulations and endangering the safety of their guests. Some Airbnb hosts complain that they are not able to receive compensation for vandalism or theft. In many countries, a shared economy, like the example of Airbnb, currently exists in a grey area between legal and illegal.

共享經濟

共享經濟又稱作合作經濟，經常以社群媒體或其它行動資訊科技為基礎，要旨是社區成員能夠以低價或免費的方式提供商品或服務給其他成員，這樣一來，寶貴的資源會被充分使用，而不會被浪費。很多共享經濟的實踐者相信這真的會改變整個市場運作的方式。

Airbnb 為一個典型的例子，這是一個讓人登記住所，以及供人尋找、租賃住宿空間的平台，透過 Airbnb，很多背包客快速而容易地找到了房間，很多年邁夫婦提供子女留下的空房間給 Airbnb，Airbnb 鼓勵主人與客人於簡介欄留下對彼此的評語，好讓新成員瀏覽。至今有相當多關於主人與客人的良好紀錄，但是也有些意圖不良的人濫用了這個平台。

飯店業者認為 Airbnb 極度顛覆市場，他們批評 Airbnb 不遵守飯店業的行規，不顧客人的安全，有些 Airbnb 的主人抱怨房間受到破壞或竊盜時，沒有辦法獲得賠償。在許多國家裡，像 Airbnb 的共享經濟目前存在於合法與非法之間的灰色地帶。

字彙與片語

- collaborative [kə'læbərətɪv] a. 合作的
- accommodation [ə,kɑmə'deʃən] n. 住所

- disruptive [dɪs'rʌptɪv] a. 引起混亂的
- abide by 遵從；遵守
- vandalism ['vændlɪzəm] n. 破壞行為；破壞後果

3. Terminology 財經專業術語

sharing economy 分享經濟

　　直接與他人分享不常用的資產或服務，通常透過社群網站運作的一個經濟系統，可以付些許費用或完全免費。

access economy 使用權經濟

　　商品或服務是以使用權為基礎來交易的經濟模式，例如暫時的租賃而非永久的擁有或銷售買賣。

collaborative finance 合作財務

　　經濟行為由兩方直接進行，不再透過傳統的金融機構，這種新的經濟模式因為社群媒體的普及而更發達。

reputation capital 名譽資本

　　這是一種在社會或市場中衡量聲譽的方式，特別是指對社區的服務與質量上的貢獻，名譽資本經常為個人帶來的是社會上的尊敬，而非金錢的報酬。

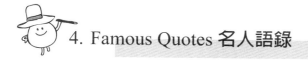

I believe we are at the start of a collaborative revolution that will be as significant as the industrial revolution.

Rachel Botsman

我相信我們正處於合作革命的開端，這將會和工業革命一樣重要。

瑞秋・波茲曼

Reputation capital will determine our access to collaborative consumption. It's a new social currency, so to speak, that could become as powerful as our credit rating.

Rachel Botsman

名譽資本會決定我們是否能夠進入合作消費，這就如同某種新型的社會貨幣，能夠變得像信用評量那樣重要。

瑞秋・波茲曼

Technologies are only as good as the political and social context in which they are employed. Software, crowdsourcing, and the information commons give us powerful tools for building social solidarity, democracy, and sustainability. Now our task is to build a movement to harness that power.

Juliet Schor

科技的好處必須要依照其所被運用的政治與社會背景而定。軟體、群眾募資，以及共同資訊為我們帶來有力的工具，可用來建立社會團結、民主、永續性，現在我們的任務是推行運動來駕馭那個力量。

　　　　　　　　　　　　　　　　　　　茱麗葉・休爾

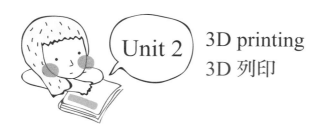

Unit 2 3D printing
3D 列印

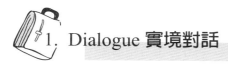

1. Dialogue 實境對話

 5-2

A: Have you heard of 3D printing?

B: I have heard of the term, but since I am not a person who enjoys building models, I don't think it has much to do with me.

A: If I told you 3D printing is now widely used in the biomedical field, would you be a bit more interested in it?

B: Really? Tell me more about it.

A: Biotechnology experts now can build vital organs and some body parts by 3D printing with human tissue.

B: Does that mean patients can make use of 3D printed implants and prosthetics?

A: That's right. Many patients can benefit much from this field of research, also called bio-printing.

B: How about healthcare products? Can they be reproduced by 3D printing?

A: Of course. Slowly and surely many devices can be easily "copied" by 3D printing computers. It will revolutionize the way people live and consume.

B: It would have a great impact on all markets.

A: That's why it is also known as the 3D revolution, which is absolutely disruptive for businesses.

中文翻譯

A： 你聽過3D列印嗎？

B： 聽過，不過既然我不是個喜歡做模型的人，3D列印與我沒有什麼很大的關係。

A： 如果我告訴你說，3D列印現在普遍用於生物醫療領域，你會比較感興趣嗎？

B： 真的？再多告訴一點關於3D列印的事。

A： 生技專家現在可以用3D列印人類組織來製成人類重要器官與身體某些部位。

B： 你的意思是說病人可以用3D列印成的植入物和義肢嗎？

A： 是的，很多病人可以從這個領域的研究當中獲益良多，也叫作生物列印。

B： 那麼健康產品呢？也可以用3D列印複製嗎？

A： 當然可以，漸漸地很多裝置都一定可以用3D列印電腦「複製」，如此一來，人們生活與消費方式都會有大改革。

B： 3D列印對所有市場都會有很大的影響。

A： 這就是為什麼3D列印又叫3D革命，這會顛覆很多產業。

字彙與片語

- biotechnology [ˌbaɪətɛk'nɑlədʒɪ] n. 生物技術；生物工程
- tissue ['tɪʃʊ] n.（動植物的）組織
- revolutionize [ˌrɛvə'luʃənˌaɪz] v. 徹底改革
- impact ['ɪmpækt] n. 衝擊、影響
- disruptive [dɪs'rʌptɪv] a. 引起混亂的

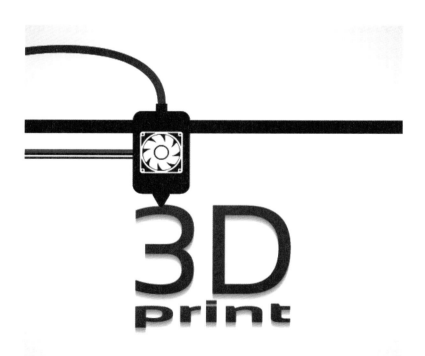

3D Printing

3D printing is also known as additive manufacturing. It is a process of using computers to make three-dimensional solid objects. Layers are added to one another horizontally and in the end, all these thin layers create a finished product.

The technology of 3D printing can be applied in many industries. For example, in architecture, it is common to use 3D printing to build architectural models. In medicine, 3D printed implants and prosthetic parts are already utilized very widely. 3D printing can also be used in archaeology to reconstruct bones. In investigating criminal cases, 3D printing is very useful in forensic evidence reconstruction. It can also be used for personal and business purposes, such as recreating memorable items or toys, and in the entertainment industry, making props for a film.

The outlook of 3D printing technology is very promising. In the foreseeable future, many major industries are expected to be transformed by this technological revolution.

本文翻譯

3D 列印

3D列印又稱積層製造，這是用電腦來製造三度空間實體的過程，一層一層的薄層平行堆疊而累積起來，最後組合成一個完工的產品。

　　3D 列印這項科技可以應用於很多產業，例如在建築業，用 3D 列印來製造建築模型非常常見；在醫療產業，使用 3D 列印製成的植入物和義肢已經非常普遍；3D 列印也可以用於考古學的骨骼重建；調查犯罪案子時，3D 列印對法醫證據的重建非常有用；3D 也可以用於個人與商業用途，例如重建富有意義的物品或玩具，還有製作娛樂業的電影道具。

　　3D 列印的前景很為人看好，在可預見的將來，很多主流產業都預期會受到這項科技革命而產生大轉變。

字彙與片語

- three-dimensional ['θridə'mɛnʃənəl] a. 三維的；立體的；三度的
- layer ['leɚ] n. 層；階層
- horizontally [ˌhɑrə'zɑntˌlɪ] adv. 水平地
- implant [ɪm'plænt] n. 植入物
- prosthetic [prɑs'θɛtɪk] a. 義肢的，假體的
- utilize ['jutˌaɪz] v. 利用
- prop [prɑp] n. 道具

3. Terminology 財經專業術語

additive manufacturing (AM)　積層製造

又稱為加法式製造，此為描述 3D 產品形成過程的正確科技用法，亦即不斷增加一層又一層的材料來製作立體產品，例如塑膠、金屬、混凝土等等。

mass customization　大量客製化

大量客製化為電腦輔助的製造系統，能大幅減低大量生產所需的費用，並且因應個別客戶的需求做彈性的客製化服務。

digital modeling and fabrication　數位化造型與製造

這是以 3D 造型軟體或電腦輔助設計軟體，將設計與製造結合起來的過程。如此一來，設計師能製造數位化的立體產品，比從前的電腦圖像來得更為精確。

4. Famous Quotes 名人語錄

Similar to computer technology in the '60s, 3D printing is a universal technology that has the potential to revolutionize our life by enabling individuals to design and manufacture things.

Hod Lipson

類似 60 年代的電腦科技，3D 列印是全球性的科技，具有全面改變我們生活的潛能，能讓個人設計並製造物品。

霍德‧黎普森

....

We are enormously proud to be the first to deliver a truly affordable 3D printing solution to our customers, one that will no doubt go a long way towards improving our customer's bottom line.

Abe Reichental

我們對於能首次提供真正平價的 3D 列印技術深感驕傲，這樣的技術一定可以大幅減少我們顧客為此需付的費用。

安北‧瑞千塔

Unit 3 Drones and Driverless Cars
無人機和無人車

1. Dialogue 實境對話

 5-3

A: Did you know that Amazon is testing the use of drones to deliver goods?

B: Do you mean those flying objects controlled remotely by a computer?

A: Exactly. They are supposed to take over the work of delivery businesses.

B: I saw on TV that the drones caused many accidents and sometimes failed to accomplish their mission.

A: Maybe the artificial intelligence used in this field simply has to be improved.

B: I heard in the military and in the field of navigation, they already have similar drones, sophisticated enough to carry out all tasks.

A: You are probably right. I think scientists and researchers will soon come up with smart drones to deliver goods to our front doors.

B: But would you like to get your birthday gifts delivered by a drone?

A: It might not be as nice as by a delivery man, but a drone can work regardless of the weather.

B: I don't think I could ever get used to receiving a parcel from a drone.

A: Why is that?

B: Where am I supposed to sign to show I got it?

A: Maybe all you have to do is to press a small button.

B: Just think about what else a drone can do. It might collect all the data about my place and its surroundings. That sounds creepy.

中文翻譯

A： 你知道亞馬遜正在測試無人機送貨碼？

B： 你是說那些電腦遙控的飛行物體嗎？

A： 沒錯，聽說他們會取代物流業送貨的工作。

B： 我在電視上看到無人機引起很多意外事故，有時無法達成使命。

A： 或許這方面所使用的人工智慧有待改善。

B： 我聽說在軍事和航海領域，他們已經有類似的無人機，精密到能完成所有任務。

A： 可能你說的對。我想科學家和研究人員很快就會發明聰明的無人機，可以送貨到府。

B： 不過，你會想要無人機為你送生日禮物來嗎？

A： 無人機或許比不上送貨人員，但是無人機可以在任何天候下運作。

B： 我想我很難適應要從無人機那兒收到包裹。

A： 為什麼呢？

B： 我該要在哪邊簽名表示收到了呢？

A： 或許只需要按個小按鈕。

B： 想想無人機還可能會做什麼？無人機可能會收集我的住所和周遭的數據資料，聽起來真可怕。

字彙與片語

- drone [dron] n. 無人機
- remotely [rɪ'motlɪ] adv. 遠距離地；遙遠地
- navigation [ˌnævə'geʃən] n. 航海；航空；航行
- sophisticated [sə'fɪstɪˌketɪd] a. 精密的，高度發展的
- creepy ['kripɪ] a. 令人毛骨悚然的；不寒而慄的

Driverless Cars

Machines play a vital role in the industry of transportation, just as they do in many other businesses. Driverless cars are being developed by the world's leading auto companies. Some experts in this field believe in the future humans will have more important things to do than driving and will, therefore, depend on driverless cars.

Some good characteristics of driverless cars are that they can drive, brake and park better than human drivers. Their automatic systems can better detect danger in traffic and can guarantee passengers more safety than our traditional cars and drivers. Automobiles equipped with artificial intelligence are regarded as useful tools for people with disabilities and may have a future as driverless taxis and for military defense purposes.

The major barriers facing cars not driven by people are the legal issues. What if the self-braking system does not work and results in a terrible traffic accident with deaths? Are the auto industries ready to insure their driverless cars or cabs? How would all these impact the existing traffic regulations? Many aspects involving technology and law-making are yet to be researched in this particular case.

本文翻譯

無人車

就像在其它產業一樣，機器人在運輸業中也扮演重要的角色。世界頂尖的汽車公司正在研發無人車。有些這方面的專家相信，未來人們會有比開車更重要的事要做，因此會依賴無人車。

無人車在開車、煞車、停車方面比真人駕駛做得更好，這是無人車的優點。他們的自動系統比起傳統車子與駕駛較能偵測到交通的危險狀況，較能夠確保行人的安全。有人工智慧配備的汽車被視為有益身心障礙者的工具，還可能可以當未來的無人計程車，甚至用於軍事防禦用途方面。

無人駕駛的汽車所面臨的最大障礙為法律問題。要是自動煞車系統失靈導致交通事故發生該怎麼辦？汽車業是否準備好要為他們的無人車與無人計程車投保？這些對既有交通規則會有什麼影響？在這一方面，很多關於科技與立法問題仍有待研討。

字彙與片語

- automatic [ˌɔtə'mætɪk] a. 自動的，自動裝置的
- detect [dɪ'tɛkt] v. 發現，察覺；查出
- guarantee [ˌɡærən'ti] v. 保證
- passenger ['pæsndʒɚ] n. 乘客，旅客
- barrier ['bærɪr] n. 障礙，阻礙

3. Terminology 財經專業術語

self-driving vehicles 無人駕駛汽車

無人駕駛汽車也稱無人車、智能車、無人自動駕駛車、自主導航車，是室外移動機器人在交通領域的重要應用。無人駕駛車系統是一個集環境感知、規劃決策和多等級輔助駕駛等功能於一體的綜合系統，是充分考慮車路合一、協調規劃的車輛系統，也是智能交通系統的重要組成部分。

artificial intelligence (AI) 人工智慧

英文縮寫爲 AI。它是研究、開發用於模擬和擴展人的智能的理論、方法、技術及應用系統的一門新的技術科學。人工智慧是計算機科學的一個分支，它企圖了解智能的實質，並生產出一種新的能以人類智能相似的方式作出反應的智能機器，該領域的研究包括機器人、語言識別、圖像識別、自然語言處理、專家系統等。

home delivery 宅配

將指定的產品在指定的時間內送到指定地點的服務。宅配送也叫宅配，起源於日本以「宅急便」爲名稱的送貨到家的服務，這種物流模式延伸到各項零售產品的銷售。

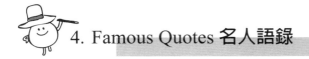

This is a disruptive technology. Literally anyone can now crop scout with a drone, and get actionable data in minutes.

Iain Butler

這是一種顛覆性的科技。真的,現在任何人都可以架設無人機來做偵測,而且在幾分鐘內獲得極為有用的數據資料。

宜安 • 巴特勒

I do not say drones have only killed civilians. They would have or might have killed some militants. But overall, they have killed mostly civilians who have nothing to do with what America is trying to do in Pakistan or Afghanistan or anywhere else in the world.

Faheem Qureshi

我並不是說無人機只造成了平民的死亡。無人機可能已經導致,或差點造成一些軍人的死亡。只不過就整體來說,美國的無人機在巴基斯坦或阿富汗或世上其它地方,已經讓許多無辜平民賠上性命。

法荷恩 • 奎瑞希

Some Google employees have their self-driving vehicles take them to work. These car robots don't look like something from 'The Jetsons'; the driverless features on these cars are a bunch of sensors, wires, and software. This technology 'works.'

　　有些谷歌員工讓自駕車載他們去工作，這些汽車機器人看起來不像「傑森一家」裡的玩意，這些無人車的特色爲一堆感應器、電線、軟體，真的是能夠運作的科技。

泰勒‧寇恩

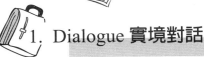

Unit 4 Wearable Technology
穿戴式科技

1. Dialogue 實境對話   5-4

A: Have you heard of wearable devices such as fitness trackers?

B: Is that some sort of gadget you put on to measure your health?

A: Yes, they can measure heart rate, blood pressure, step counts and so on, especially while you are doing exercise.

B: Don't the activity trackers have to be connected to smart phones?

A: That's right. At the moment, they still have to rely on mobile smart phones or tablets, which can scan the wearable devices and show the data on the screen.

B: I assume the results of such health checks can be sent to family members or doctors immediately.

A: Yes, it has already been done with some chronic illness patients. These mobile health trackers can detect emergent symptoms and save time in rescuing patients.

B: What concerns me here are the privacy issues. Don't users of wearable devices feel they are being monitored all the time?

A: Of course, the fitness trackers have to be used with the agreement of the users and their care-takers.

B: For many patients, it means life or death to wear these health trackers.

A: In the current market, some of the most common mobile activity trackers are those which help manage weight, stress, sleep and physical fitness.

B: They seem to be personal health monitors that everyone can find useful in daily life.

中文翻譯

A： 你聽過像是健康追蹤手帶那樣的穿戴式裝置嗎？

B： 是不是像是戴來測量健康狀況的配備？

A： 是的，可以用來測量心跳、血壓、步數等等，特別是在做運動時。

B： 這種活動紀錄器難道不需要與智慧型手機相連結嗎？

A： 需要，現在還是需要依賴智慧型手機或平板來掃描穿戴式裝置，並且於螢幕上呈現數據資料。

B： 我推測這些健康檢查的結果可以馬上傳給家人或醫師。

A： 對，某些慢性病人已經這麼做了，這些行動的健康紀錄器可以偵測到緊急症狀，節省急救病人的時間。

B： 令我擔心的是隱私權問題，穿戴式裝置的使用者不會感到一直被監控嗎？

A： 當然，使用者與看護者在使用健康追蹤器時要簽同意書。

B： 對很多人來說，戴這種健康紀錄器可是生死攸關。

A： 在現今的市場，最流行的活動紀錄器是可以管理體重、壓力、睡眠、體能狀況的配備。

B： 似乎是每個人於日常生活都可以用得上的健康追蹤器。

字彙與片語

- tracker ['trækɚ] n. 追蹤器
- assume [ə'sjum] v. 以為；假定為
- chronic ['krɑnɪk] a. （病）慢性的；（人）久病的
- rescue ['rɛskju] v. 援救；營救；挽救

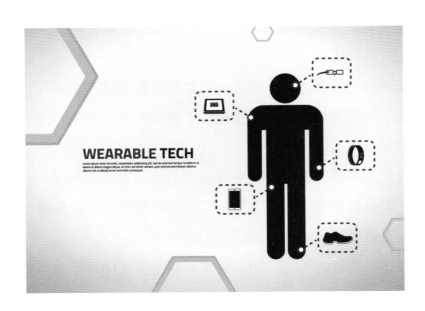

Wearable Technology

In recent years, wearable activity trackers have become quite popular, and some of them are equipped with augmented reality to provide supplemental information, such as graphics. These devices are mainly used to monitor the user's health conditions, like heart rate, body temperature and stress level.

One of the most useful features is that the users can wear the personal activity trackers while doing sports or walking or sleeping. There is no need to switch on and off the devices, which can constantly record the user's health data. What's more, these wearable fitness trackers or wristbands, with electronics, software and sensors, do not interfere with the user's activities at all. In this sense, they are like an extension of the user's body or brain.

Currently, wearable fitness trackers still have to be connected to smart phones or other digital devices, which means users have to carry and recharge at least two electronic tools if they want to use them outdoors. Overall, wearable technology is a booming business, whether for personal or commercial use. Once the technology has improved and the prices have become affordable, its future markets will be unlimited.

穿戴式科技

近幾年來，穿戴式的活動紀錄器變得相當流行，有些還有擴增實境的配備來提供補充資料，例如圖表。這些裝備主要用於衡量使用者的健康狀況，例如心跳、體溫、壓力等級。

最有用的特色之一是，使用者能在做運動時或走路或睡眠時，戴著個人的活動紀錄器，不需要將配備打開或關起來，就可以不斷紀錄使用者的健康數據資料。更好的一點是，這些穿戴式的活動紀錄器或手帶，附有電子、軟體、感應器，一點也不會影響使用者的活動，如此一來，就像是使用者身體或頭腦的延伸。

目前穿戴式的活動紀錄器仍然需要和智慧型手機或其它數位配備相結合，這代表如果使用者要在戶外使用，必須攜帶至少兩個電子工具，還要充電。整體來說，不論是個人或商業用途，穿戴式科技的前景看好，只要科技獲得改進，價格變得較平價，未來的市場將無可限量。

字彙與片語

- supplemental [ˌsʌpləˈmɛnt!] a. 補充的
- extension [ɪkˈstɛnʃən] n. 延長部分
- recharge [riˈtʃɑrdʒ] v. 再充電於

- booming ['bumɪŋ] a. 興旺發達的；景氣好的；大受
  歡迎的
- affordable [ə'fɔrdəb!] a. 負擔得起的

3. Terminology 財經專業術語

▼ virtual reality (VR) 虛擬實境

　　虛擬實境的基本原理是利用電腦與其他特殊硬設備（如顯像式頭盔、3D 音響、遊戲裝置等）及電腦軟體，模擬三度空間環境，讓使用者於此虛擬世界與電腦互動，進入虛擬的世界，彷彿身歷其境般。

▼ augmented reality (AR) 增強現實

　　也被稱為混合現實，它是在虛擬現實的基礎上發展起來的新興技術，用戶可以在真實場景上，看到由電腦等科學技術例如感應器，所生成模擬仿真的虛擬景象。

▼ activity tracker 活動記錄器

　　這是一種可以測量體能的隨身裝置，可以用於走路或跑步，還有其他的各種運動，所記錄的項目包含有所燃燒的卡路里、心跳、睡眠品質等等。

4. Famous Quotes 名人語錄

This wearable technology space is going to become an emerging trend. As we look at different people and the way they integrate technology into their lives to stay connected, it's really finally coming together across the board with products from a whole range of industries. The key is not just throwing the technology in there, but making sure it's easy to use and something the audience can relate to.

Scott Martin

這種穿戴式科技的空間會成為一股新興的趨勢,我們看各種人他們將科技融入生活中,藉此與別人保持連繫,這真的是將各產業的產品聯合起來。關鍵在於並非光有科技,而是確定科技容易使用,與大眾生活有關係。

史考特 · 馬汀

From wearable sensors to video game treatments, everyone seems to be looking to technology as the next wave of innovation for mental health care.

Thomas R. Insel

從穿戴式感應器到電玩特別裝置,大家似乎都將科技視為心理健康照護的下一波創新。

湯瑪斯 · 爾 · 因塞耳

With the advent of wearable technology, companies will soon be able to better provide ads to customers based on their real-time activity.

Robert Scoble

隨著穿戴式科技的來臨，企業很快就能依照消費者的真實行為來提供更好的廣告。

羅柏特・史寇伯

. . . .

Doing exercise without monitoring yourself will be rare in the future of wearable technology.

Astro Teller

在未來的穿戴式科技時代，從事運動而沒有隨時衡量自己狀況，這會非常罕見。

亞斯楚・特勒

Urban Renewal
都市更新

1. Dialogue 實境對話 🎧 5-5

A: Have you heard of urban renewal?

B: I think I have, but I don't know what it is exactly. Is it about making an old community new again?

A: You can put it that way. It is also called "urban regeneration," such as the case of Dadaocheng.

B: The other day I went to Dadaocheng with my friends from Japan and found many interesting stores over there.

A: What kinds of stores are you talking about?

B: There is this tea shop in an old renovated house, which looks full of history.

A: What else have you seen in that neighborhood?

B: There are boutiques where souvenirs like bags and shirts are sold. They are called products of the Cultural and Creative Industry.

A: I bet they have the beautiful scenery of Dadaocheng on them.

B: In some of these places, you can even attend DIY workshops and make something yourself.

A: Many parents would love to take their kids there to create things together.

B: Particularly when the Lunar New Year is approaching, many people go there for their yearly shopping to prepare for the festive holidays.

A: At the moment, Dihua Street must be full of locals and tourists hanging out there.

B: The old and the new elements seem to mix quite well in this renewed area.

A: All of these businesses can definitely revive the once seemingly old community.

B: As long as they keep bringing up new ideas for this unique neighborhood.

中文翻譯

A： 你聽過都市更新嗎？

B： 聽過，但是我不知道那確切是什麼，是將老社區重新變成新的嗎？

A： 你可以這麼說，都市更新也叫作「都市再生」，像是大稻埕的例子。

B： 前幾天我和日本的朋友去大稻埕，發現了那兒有很多有意思的店家。

A： 你指的是怎麼樣的店家呢？

B： 有家茶店位在修復好的古屋內，看起來很有歷史感。

A： 你在那個社區還看見了什麼？

B： 有些精品店，賣像是袋子和 T 恤的紀念品，他們稱之為文化創意產品。

A： 我猜上面都印有大稻埕的美景。

B： 在有的店家，你還可以參加手作工作坊，自己動手做。

A： 很多家長會想要帶小孩到那兒，一起創作。

B： 特別是在農曆新年來時，很多人都會去那邊採買年貨。

A： 現在迪化街一定到處是逛街的本地人與觀光客。

B： 舊元素與新元素似乎在這個更新地區融合得相當不錯。

A： 所有這些商業一定可以重振這個似乎看來沒落的老社區。

B： 只要業者能不斷將新點子帶進這個獨特的社區。

字彙與片語

- renewal [rɪ'njuəl] n. 更新；復原；恢復
- regeneration [rɪ,dʒɛnə'reʃən] n. 恢復；新生；革新；復興
- renovate ['rɛnə,vet] v. 更新；重做
- revive [rɪ'vaɪv] v. 甦醒；復甦
- seemingly ['simɪŋlɪ] adv. 表面上；似乎是

Urban Renewal

Urban renewal is a process of land redevelopment in an urban area. Very often it involves the government purchase of private property for public land projects. Inevitably, this causes the demolition of many old existing buildings, and the relocation of residents and businesses.

Some regard urban renewal as a way to boost the economy and to recreate old communities; others criticize it for destroying the old structures and thus the authentic local culture. The local government plays a key role in the whole process. Experts of city planning are frequently invited to discuss the possible development plans with the local business owners and to find ways to minimize the damages to the community.

The aim of urban renewal programs is to revitalize old communities and to encourage business investments in old neighborhoods. The renovation of the heritage buildings reflects the preservation of local traditional culture. More and more, residents of urban renewal areas do not want to sacrifice their historical architecture in order to have economic gains.

都市更新

都市更新為都市土地重新發展的過程，經常會牽涉到政府買私人土地，來作為公共土地用途，無可避免地會拆毀很多既有建築，造成住民和商業的遷移。

有些人將都市更新視為振興經濟的方法，以重建老社區；有些人則批評都市更新會破壞老建築，因此毀壞當地真正道地的文化。當地政府在整個過程中扮演關鍵的角色，都市計劃專家經常會受邀來與當地業主討論可能的發展計劃，找出降低對社區造成傷害的方法。

都市更新計劃的目的是為了要活化舊社區，鼓勵對老社區的商業投資，古蹟建築的翻修反映出地方傳統文化，越來越多都市更新地區的居民不希望犧牲古蹟建物來獲得商業利益。

字彙與片語

- inevitably [ɪn'ɛvətəblɪ] adv. 不可避免地；必然地
- demolition [ˌdɛmə'lɪʃən] n. 破壞；毀壞
- authentic [ɔ'θɛntɪk] a. 可信的，真實的，可靠的
- minimize ['mɪnəˌmaɪz] v. 使減到最少，使縮到最小
- revitalize [ri'vaɪt!ˌaɪz] v. 使恢復生氣；使復活；使復興

3. Terminology 財經專業術語

gentrification　仕紳化

是 20 世紀 60 年代末西方發達國家城市中心區更新過程中出現的一種社會空間現象，其特徵是城市中產階級以上階層取代低收入階級重新由郊區返回城市中心區。

community development　社區發展

社區發展是指在城鄉基層社區中社區居民依靠社區自身力量，在政府和其他組織機構的支持下，推動社區有計劃的社會變遷，改善社區的經濟、社會、文化狀況，提高社區居民的生活品質。

urban economic circle　城市經濟圈

以一個或多個經濟較發達並具有較強城市功能的中心城市為核心，包括與其有經濟聯繫的若干周邊城鎮，其經濟吸引力和經濟影響力能夠達到，並能促進相應地區經濟發展的最大地域範圍。

4. Famous Quotes 名人語錄

The word 'gentrification' is an expression of social inequality that attempts to describe the relationship between profit and exploitation with regards to land.

Kate Shaw

「仕紳化」這個字代表了社會的不平等，所試圖描述的是關於土地的利益和剝削之間的關係。

凱特 · 蕭

....

There are degrees which you can choose to gentrify a neighbourhood ... all developments are the result of choices.

Kate Shaw

仕紳化一個地區，有很多程度供選擇……所有的開發皆是選擇的結果。

凱特 · 蕭

....

When people talk about gentrification they are talking about a variety of urban processes and using it as an umbrella term.

Heidi Seetzan

當人們談到「仕紳化」，他們所談的是各種不同的都更過程，全都概括在這個廣義名詞的含義之下。

海蒂 · 蔡贊

....

We hear nothing from the local residents ... what we get is interviews with the cafe owners, who are seen as the victims and the authority on the matter. That is the problem.

Lisa McKenzie

我們沒有聽到當地居民的任何意見……我們看到的是，看似受害者的咖啡屋業主和地方當局在接受訪問，這就是問題癥結所在。

麗莎・麥肯茲

Chapter 6 Vision

願景

Unit 1 Synergy
合作效應

1. Dialogue 實境對話 6-1

A: I've noticed that you seldom ask for help from your colleagues, even in a joint project.

B: It doesn't mean that I do not enjoy working with others; it means I respect others' time.

A: Working together with others often brings about the best end results.

B: I know, but I find sometimes it saves me a lot of time to carry out my own plan.

A: It is nice that you do not mind putting in more effort, but communication between you and your coworkers is as important as the joint effort.

B: I know what you mean.

A: You have been working in this company for such a long time that you should know what to say to make your colleagues do their jobs well.

B: You are perfectly right. Some young newcomers seem to lack motivation and passion, and I let them get away with it. Maybe it's because I am just not tough by nature.

A: In the next major project, I'll designate you as the project manager to lead a team.

B: Then I'll have the authority to persuade my colleagues to be better team players than before.

中文翻譯

A： 我注意到你很少向你的同事求助，即使是團隊專案也一樣。

B： 這並不代表我不喜歡與別人共事；代表的是我尊重別人的時間。

A： 與別人共同合作經常會帶來最好的結果。

B： 我知道，但是我發現有時自己來進行我自己的計劃可以省下很多時間。

A： 你不介意投入更多的心力固然很好，但是與同事之間的溝通與團隊合作一樣重要。

B： 我知道你的意思。

A： 你在這家公司工作了這麼久，你應該知道該說什麼來使你的同事做他們該做的事。

B： 你說的很對，有些年輕的新進人員似乎缺乏動力與熱情，我沒對他們特別要求，或許這是因為我天生就不夠強悍吧。

A： 在下個專案，我會指定你當專案經理來帶領一個團隊。

B： 那麼我就會有說服我的同事的職權，能使我的同事在團隊中比從前表現得更好。

- synergy ['sɪnɚdʒɪ] n. 合作效應；合力，協力
- joint [dʒɔɪnt] a. 合辦的，共有的
- motivation [,motə'veʃən] n. 動機
- passion ['pæʃən] n. 熱情，激情
- designate ['dɛzɪɡ,net] v. 指定

Synergy

Synergy is the extra energy or effectiveness that people or businesses create when they work together. In business, profitability is often expected to benefit from the combination of two efforts. Man power is another term for synergy, which sounds quite appropriate to describe the collaboration among people of various backgrounds and skills.

In reality, few people can tackle all tasks alone at one time; team work is therefore inevitable. Of course, efficiency in communication is vital to make synergy work. Thanks to information technology, transparency is, to a great extent, improved. It is quite common for the employees at the bottom of a company to voice their opinions, which can be received in an instant. Many subordinates feel very empowered in the process of such communication and are more willing to participate in monitoring the operation of their organizations.

Leadership is extremely vital in combining joint efforts, especially in the business world where mergers and acquisitions constantly take place. Management becomes more challenging than ever in the process of achieving synergy and creating man power.

本文翻譯

合作效應

合作效應指的是人們或企業合作所產生的額外能量或效能，人們常期待商業的獲利性會因結合兩方的力量而增加。合作效應又名人力資源，聽起來相當適於描述不同背景與技能的人在一起的團隊合作。

事實上，很少人能夠單打獨鬥，因此少不了團隊合作。當然，溝通的效率是使合作效應發生的關鍵。因為科技發達，透明化已大幅改善。經常可以見到，公司底層的員工一發表意見，馬上就會被接收到。很多下屬感到這樣的溝通過程授與他們很大的權力，變得更願意參與檢察他們組織的運作。

領導力在連結力量時極為重要，特別是在併購不斷發生的商業界，管理的挑戰性在獲得合作效應與人力資源的過程中變得無比的高。

字彙與片語

- effectiveness [ɛ'fɛktɪvnɪs] n. 有效；有力
- profitability [ˌprɑfɪtə'bɪlətɪ] n. 利潤率；收益性
- appropriate [ɛ'proprɪˌet] a. 適當的，恰當的，相稱的
- tackle ['tæk!] v. 處理

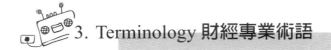
3. Terminology 財經專業術語

synergy　合作效應
　　合作效應又稱加乘性、協助作用、協助效應、協同作用、加成作用、加乘作用，指「一加一大於二」的效應，例如商業環境，市場或企業合併或收購，有可能產生互補不足或相輔相成的合作效應。

teamwork　團隊合作
　　團隊合作是指一群人為相同目標而組成團隊合力工作的概念。團隊合作一般被認為比獨自工作更有效率，因此招聘員工時，通常會要求應徵者具有團隊合作的精神和能力。

team spirit　團隊精神
　　團隊精神也稱為士氣，是指一個團隊的工作氣勢和氛圍，它用來描述個體或群體在維護共同信仰和目標時，表現出來的努力、鬥志和效率。團隊精神一詞適用於軍隊或團隊運動的成員，也適用於商業或任何其他組織方面，特別是在壓力和爭議下所展現出來的氣勢，更準確的話，則是個人在集體利益下所展示的信念、心態、動機。

4. Famous Quotes 名人語錄

I still believe in synergy, but I call it natural law.

Barry Diller

我仍然相信同心協力，只不過我稱之為自然定律。

巴里・迪勒

....

When it all boils down, it's about embracing each others' stories and maybe even finding that synergy to collaborate for the common good.

Dhani Jones

總而言之，就是要擁抱每個人的故事，或甚至找到為了共同利益的合作關係。

達尼・瓊斯

....

I truly believe in positive synergy, that your positive mindset gives you a more hopeful outlook, and belief that you can do something great means you will do something great.

Russell Wilson

我真的相信正面的合作力量，你的正面觀點會帶給你較有希望的看法，相信你能成就大事的想法真能讓你成就大事。

盧梭・威爾森

....

Synergy is what happens when one plus one equals ten or a hundred or even a thousand! It's the profound result when two or more respectful human beings determine to go beyond their preconceived ideas to meet a great challenge.

Stephen Covey

　　同心合作是一加一等於十或一百或甚至一千！這是兩個或多個受尊重的人決定一起突破先前的成見，面對巨大挑戰的有力結果。

史蒂芬 · 柯非

Unit 2 Better Benefits for Employees
更佳的員工福利

1. Dialogue 實境對話

 6-2

A: Are you insured at your workplace?

B: Not really. This is a part-time job, and every day I work in the tea shop only for 4 or 5 hours. There seems to be no need for any insurance.

A: Have you asked for the labor insurance?

B: No, because my employer says only full-time workers can have labor insurance.

A: Why didn't you work full-time then?

B: I was told that I could only start on a part-time basis, and after a while, my boss will let me know if I can be qualified to work full-time.

A: Did you know it is against regulations to not provide labor insurance?

B: No. I think, at least, I have my own health insurance anyway.

A: How much money are you getting paid for this job?

B: 110 dollars per hour.

A: Did you know the minimum wage now is 120 dollars per hour?

B: In that case I'm ripped off!

中文翻譯

A： 你的工作有保險嗎？

B： 沒有，這是一份兼差，每天我在茶店只不過打工四五個小時，似乎不需要任何保險。

A： 你曾經要求勞保嗎？

B： 沒有，因為我的雇主說只有全職員工可以有勞保。

A： 那麼你為什麼不做全職的呢？

B： 他們告訴我只能從兼職開始，過一陣子，我的老闆才會讓我知道我是否夠資格做全職。

A： 你知道沒有勞保是違法的嗎？

B： 不知道，我想說至少我自己有健保。

A： 你這份差事的薪水多少？

B： 每小時110元。

A： 你知道現在最低薪資每小時120元嗎？

B： 那麼我被剝削了！

字彙與片語

- labor insurance 勞保
- health insurance 健保
- minimum ['mɪnəməm] a. 最低的，最少的
- ripped off 剝削

Preventive Measures against Occupational Injuries

Many employers have realized that in order to prevent employees from getting hurt in the workplace, it is important to take preventive measures. This includes dealing with employees' physical injuries and psychological problems, such as depression due to heavy workloads or stress.

Health check-ups are often provided by quite a few companies, and in some companies, doctors and consultants are employed for staff members. It is part of their work to check the employees' physical conditions and their working environments to see if there is anything that can be improved. In production lines, it is especially important to prevent the workers' physical injuries. Sometimes the workers are recommended to quit smoking or are advised to take part in workshops to learn stress management. The insurance industry is carefully studying the risks involved in various workplaces, and it is believed that for every industry there should be customized occupational hazard insurance.

The idea behind preventive measures is that before the risks actually happen, employers should take actions to prevent them from occurring, and employees also have to report signs of potential danger. In this way, both of them can work together to minimize the possible damages for which they both are likely to be held responsible.

職業災害的預防措施

很多雇主相信為了要避免員工在職場上受傷，採取預防措施非常重要，這包含處理員工的人身傷害與心理問題，例如因為工作量過大或壓力引起的憂鬱。

很多公司通常都會提供健康檢查，有的公司會為員工雇用醫師與諮商師。他們的工作包括要檢查員工的健康狀況以及工作環境來看看有什麼該改進的地方。在生產線上，預防員工身體受傷特別重要，有時候員工會被要求戒菸，或是被建議要參加壓力管理工作坊。保險業正在仔細研究各種工作場所牽涉到的危機，一般相信每種產業都必須要有客製化的職災保險。

預防措施的理念是要雇主在危機發生前就採取行動來避免危險發生，雇員也必須要報告潛在的危險徵兆。如此一來，雙方才能共同合作，以減輕雙方可能都會需要負責的傷害。

字彙與片語

- preventive [prɪ'vɛntɪv] a. 預防的；防病的
- measure ['mɛʒɚ] n. 措施；手段；方法
- occupational [,ɑkjə'peʃən!] a. 職業的
- recommend [,rɛkə'mɛnd] v. 建議，勸告；推薦

- customized [ˈkʌstəmaɪzd] a. 客製化的
- hazard [ˈhæzɚd] n. 危險；危險之源

3. Terminology 財經專業術語

performance bonus　績效獎金

　　是指由於員工達到某一績效，企業為了激勵員工這種行為而支付的獎金。當然，績效獎也包括金錢和非金錢的獎勵，每個人心目中所嚮往的東西都不一樣，所以，績效獎的實施方案也千變萬化。

industry-academy cooperation　產學合作

　　產學合作是指企業與技術學院、大專院校之間的合作，通常指以企業為技術需求方，以技術學院、大專院校為技術供給方之間的合作，其實質是促進技術創新所需各種生產要素的有效組合。

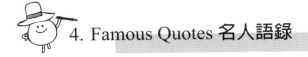

Don't organize for any other purpose than mutual benefit to the employer and the employee.

Mark Hanna

組織之目的不是爲了別的，就是爲了雇主與員工之間的共同利益。

馬克 • 漢那

. . . .

Most bosses know instinctively that their power depends more on employee's compliance than on threats or sanctions.

Fernanda Bartolme

大部分老闆會直覺地明白他們的權力建立於員工的服從，而非對員工的威脅或制裁。

費南達 • 巴爾托美

. . . .

Work/life benefits allow companies meaningful ways for responding to their employees' needs; they can be a powerful tool for transforming a workforce and driving a business' success.

Anne Mulcahy

工作／生活福利使公司能對員工的需要做出有意義的回應；同時也能夠當作是改變工作場所和驅動企業成功的有力工具。

安娜・牧爾卡伊

. . . .

I see a future where states compete with one another to see which can be the most efficient, and where businesses seek out efficient states in which to locate so they can reap the economic and environmental benefits for their businesses and employees.

Bernie Sanders

在我所看見的未來裡，州與州之間會互相競爭，看哪一州最有效率，而企業則會尋找最有效率的一州來落腳，好讓他們的公司與員工都能從經濟與環境的好處中獲利。

柏尼・桑德爾斯

Unit 3　Young Start-up Entrepreneur Program 青年創業計劃

1. Dialogue 實境對話　♪ 6-3

A: Look at this column in the newspaper. I think you should sign up for this young start-up entrepreneur program!

B: What makes you think I would be the right candidate for this program?

A: Read the requirements here: under age 35, full of innovative business ideas, fluent English, extensive understanding of international commerce and so on.

B: You know that I do not have any capital to start any business of my own, right?

A: Have you heard of crowdfunding?

B: No. What is it?

A: Crowdfunding is the practice of raising money from crowds of people, usually via the Internet.

B: Why would complete strangers be willing to invest in my start-up company?

A: If your vision for your enterprise is for the well-being of society as a whole, there will be interested business people or foundations.

B: But I am just a freelance graphic designer that gets outsourcing jobs here and there.

A: That's why I think you can benefit a lot from learning entrepreneurship in this young start-up entrepreneur program. Remember that if you get in, you can get advice and consultation for no cost at all. All you have to do is to submit your short biography and start-up business proposal.

B: That sounds fantastic. By the way, why is this program free of charge?

A: As you would imagine, this program is also supported by crowdfunding, a form of "alternative finance."

中文翻譯

A： 你看報紙的這一欄，我認為你該登記參加這個年輕新創企業家培育計劃！

B： 為什麼你會認為我是這個計劃的最佳人選呢？

A： 看這邊的要求條件：35歲以下，充滿商業點子，流利的英文與對國際商務的深度了解等等。

B： 你知道我沒有任何創業的資金吧？

A： 你聽過群眾募資吧？

B： 沒聽過，那是什麼？

A： 群眾募資就是向大眾募款，通常透過網路。

B： 素昧平生的人為何會願意貢投資我的新創公司？

A： 如果你的企業的願景是為了增進全社會的福祉，一定會有對此有
興趣的人或基金會。

B： 但是我只不過是個接案的平面設計師，到處接點外包工作罷了。

A： 這也就是我認為這個青年創業計劃對你會有很大幫助的原因。要
記住，只要你被選上就可以獲得完全免費的建議與諮詢，你只需
要繳交個人簡介與創業提案。

B： 聽起來好極了。對了，為什麼這個培育計劃免費呢？

A： 如同你可想見的，這個培育計劃也是靠群眾募資的，一種「另類
財務」的形式。

字彙與片語

- start-up ['stɑrtˌʌp] a. 開始階段的

- entrepreneur [ˌɑntrəprə'nɜ˞] n. 企業家；事業創辦者

- capital ['kæpət!] n. 資本；本錢

- crowdfunding 群眾募資；網路募捐

- proposal [prə'poz!] n. 提議；計畫；提案

Mentorship for Start-up Entrepreneurs

In almost every trade of business, finding the right people to be one's own mentors plays a decisive role in professional careers. Not all people on the top of their professions are keen on passing their knowhow and experience on to young start-up entrepreneurs. Besides, with the rapid progress in information technology, more and more beginners are not sure if they can rely on the old-fashioned ways of their predecessors.

Female start-up entrepreneurs often encounter more difficulties than their male counterparts because many of them are not conscious of their gender, and they seek advice from predominantly male mentors that can only provide them with limited help. Many successful female professionals do not necessarily like to give mentorship to female start-ups. For one thing, it is widely believed that females run their businesses differently than males. By the time females reach the executive level, their ways of thinking and handling things have become similar to their male counterparts' ways.

Being a mentor has never been an easy task, and after all, it is up to their followers to decide if their mentors are being successful and helpful. Hopefully, start-up entrepreneurs can remember what their mentors teach them and pass it on to their followers if they themselves become mentors someday.

新創企業家的師徒導師制

在幾乎所有的產業裡，能找到對的人當自己的導師對事業發展有決定性的影響。並非所有表現最傑出的人都熱衷於將他們的知識與經驗傳給年輕的新創企業家。除此之外，隨著資訊科技的快速進步，越來越多新人不太確定是否能夠依賴前輩舊式的作法。

女性新創企業家遇到的困難經常比男性多，因為很多女性年輕企業家沒有意識到男女性別差異，大多求教於男性導師，而只能得到有限的幫助。許多成功的女性專業人才並不一定會喜歡當女性新創企業家的導師，其中有個原因，很多人相信女性經營企業的方式不同於男性，等到女性到達了主管階級，她們的想法和做法已經變得與男性相似。

當導師並不容易，畢竟，導師是否成功，是否有助益，極大成分是由他們的徒弟來定義。希望新創企業家有一天自己成為導師時，能記得從前他們的導師所教導的，並且傳給接班人。

字彙與片語

- mentor ['mɛntɚ] n. 導師
- decisive [dɪ'saɪsɪv] a. 決定性的，決定的
- conscious ['kɑnʃəs] a. 意識到的，覺察到的

- executive [ɪgˈzɛkjʊtɪv] a. 經理人員的；主管級的
- counterpart [ˈkaʊntɚˌpɑrt] n. 對應的人（或物）

3. Terminology 財經專業術語

entrepreneurship　企業家精神

　　企業家精神是指企業家組織建立和經營管理企業的綜合才能的表述方式，它是一種重要而特殊的特質。

mentor program　導師計劃

　　導師計劃是指組織中較富有經驗的或績效較高的資深員工，對經驗不足的員工進行指導或培育新人，在大多數情況下，指導關係都是由於指導者和被指導者具有共同的興趣或價值觀而以一種非正式的形式形成的。

4. Famous Quotes 名人語錄

Entrepreneurship, entrepreneurship, entrepreneurship. It drives everything: Job creation, poverty alleviation, innovation.

Elliott Bisnow

　　創業，創業，創業，創業推動了每件事：創造就業機會、減輕貧窮、創新。

艾利歐特 ‧ 比斯諾

259

You know where entrepreneurship in my opinion has to go? Into the inner city.

John Kasich

你知道依我的看法，創業家精神該往哪邊發展呢？往市中心去。

約翰・卡斯許

. . . .

Entrepreneurship is not really building a product, it's not having an idea, it's not being in the right place at the right time. It's fundamentally company building.

Eric Ries

創業家精神真的不是創造一個產品，不是有個主意，不是在對的時候在對的地方，基本上創業家精神是在建立一家公司。

艾雷克・里斯

. . . .

By working to ensure we live in a society that prioritizes public safety, education, and innovation, entrepreneurship can thrive and create a better world for all of us to live in.

Ron Conway

創業家精神以確保我們能有公共安全、教育、創新為首要社會目標而努力，因此得以興盛，而且創造出更好的世界來讓我們居住。

隆・康衛

What is great about entrepreneurship is that entrepreneurs create the tangible from the intangible.

Robert Herjavec

創業家精神偉大之處在於創業家能以無形精神創造出有形資產。

羅柏特 · 赫爾札維克

Energy Issues
能源議題

1. Dialogue 實境對話 6-4

A: I heard there is an exhibition of "Green Architecture" coming to Taiwan in May. Do you want to go with me to take a look?

B: Not really. To me, most green buildings in the world are not as "green" as they claim to be.

A: What do you mean by that?

B: I read there is no widely-adopted certification system of sustainable architecture, and the existing "green" buildings cannot save as much energy as they promise.

A: Does that mean architects or industry developers can claim their buildings are very eco-friendly even though they are not really capable of saving energy?

B: I'm afraid that is what is happening now.

A: How can customers tell if they are paying for real sustainable architecture? I know that many conscientious buyers are willing to spend much more money for environmentally-friendly buildings, compared to ordinary ones.

B: They have to do some research and be informed about the architects and related issues, such as the current regulations of building materials.

A: That sounds like a lot of work because most buyers are not experts in this field.

B: That's why many buyers get ripped off by developers of such green architecture.

A: What a shame.

B: One sure thing is that green buildings should be able to provide a healthy and comfortable environment to live in, regardless of the figures of energy and water savings.

A: But that's something that you can only feel after you buy the building and move in.

B: Absolutely. You are very clever.

中文翻譯

A： 聽說有個「綠建築」展覽將於5月來台，你要跟我一起去看看嗎？

B： 不太想呢，對我而言，世上大部分綠建築都不如對外宣稱的那麼「綠」。

A： 你這話是什麼意思呢？

B： 我讀到說，廣為人接受的綠建築認證系統並不存在，而現今的「綠」建築無法如同承諾那樣節約能源。

A： 意思是不是說建築師或建商可以宣稱他們的建築物很環保，即使事實上根本不能節約能源？

B： 恐怕這樣的情形現在就正在上演。

A： 消費者要如何才能分辨他們所買的是真正永續的建築？我知道很多有良心的買家寧願多付不少錢去買相對而言較環保的建築。

B： 必須要做些研究，對於建築師與相關議題多做了解，例如現有建材的法規等等。

A： 那樣要花很多的心力，因為大多數的買家並非這領域的專家。

B： 這就是為什麼很多買家被這些綠建築建商敲詐的原因。

A： 真可惜。

B： 可以確定的一點是，綠建築必須要能提供健康與舒適的居住環境，無論節省能源與水的數據為何。

A： 但是這是買了建築物並且搬了進去，才能感覺到的事啊。

B： 完全正確，你很聰明。

字彙與片語

- exhibition [ˌɛksə'bɪʃən] n. 展覽；展覽會，展示會
- claim [klem] v. 自稱，聲稱；主張
- certification [ˌsɝtɪfə'keʃən] n. 證明；檢定；保證
- sustainable [sə'stenəb!] a. 能維持的；可持續發展的
- figure ['fɪgjɚ] n. 數字

Energy Savings in Transportation

We all know that global energy is extremely precious. Have you thought about what you can do in the area of your daily transportation to help energy savings, oil especially? The following are some tips you might find useful.

In the modern world, public transportation is usually available and affordable, so try to avoid driving a car as much as possible. Taking public transportation, like a bus or a train, can significantly reduce carbon emissions. If you do have to drive a car, make sure you drive it slowly and avoid sudden starts and braking. Turn the car off if you have to stop. In this way, you can save energy and reduce air pollution. Carpooling is always a good way to reduce the numbers of cars on the road and to save energy and cut carbon emissions.

Riding a bike is a healthy and clean way to commute to work. Walking to and from the office is even better. Another reliable way to avoid producing and breathing in air pollution is to work from home. With the advances in technology, the opportunities and possibilities in energy savings have been greatly increased.

關於運輸的節約能源

我們都知道全球能源極為珍貴,你是否曾想過你有什麼方法可以從每日的運輸當中節約能源,尤其是石油?以下的建議方法可能會對你很有用。

在當今世界,大眾公共運輸很普及且人人負擔得起,所以要盡量避免開車。搭乘公共運輸工具,像公車或火車,可以大幅減少排碳量。如果你必須要開車,務必要慢慢開,避免忽然起動與煞車。如果必須要停車,須先熄火,如此一來可以節省能源並且減少空氣汙染;共同乘車總是能夠減少路上的車輛數目,並能節能減碳。

騎腳踏車是個通勤的好方法,健康且乾淨,走路上下班更佳。還有個實用的方法來避免製造與吸入髒空氣方法是在家工作,隨著科技的進步,節省能源的機會與可能性已大幅增加。

* extremely [ɪk'strimlɪ] adv. 極其；非常
* significantly [sɪg'nɪfəkəntlɪ] adv. 顯著地
* carbon ['kɑrbən] n. 碳
* emission [ɪ'mɪʃən] n. 排放物
* carpooling 共同乘車

3. Terminology 財經專業術語

recycling　資源回收

是指收集本來要廢棄的材料，分解再製成新產品，或者是收集用過的產品，清潔、處理之後再出售。回收再利用的支持者認為這麼做可以減少垃圾，降低原料的消耗。

green energy　綠色能源

是指不排放污染物的能源，更狹義的定義是可再生能源，是指原材料可以再生的能源，如水力發電、風力發電、太陽能、生物能、地熱能、海潮能、海水溫差發電等。目前綠色能源與可再生能源幾乎是同義詞。可再生能源不存在能源耗竭的可能，因此日益受到許多國家的重視，尤其是能源短缺的國家。

green building　綠色建築

是指本身及其使用過程在生命週期中，如選址、設計、建設、營運、維護、翻新、拆除等各階段皆顧及環保與有效運用資源的一種建築。換言之，綠色建築在設計上試圖從人造建築與自然環境之間取得一個平衡點，這需要設計團隊、建築師、工程師以及客戶在專案的各階段中密切合作。

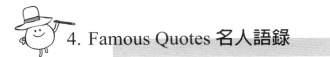

4. Famous Quotes 名人語錄

It is time, as a matter of pride, as well as a matter of national security, for the United States of America to lead the world in the energy revolution, and not lag behind Japan or Germany.

John Kerry

這是一件光榮之事，同時也事關國家安全，現在該是由美國來領導世界能源革命，不可落後於日本與德國。

約翰・凱瑞

In recent years, America's wealthiest man has begun to tackle energy issues in a major way, investing millions in everything from high-capacity batteries to machines that can scrub carbon dioxide out of the air. With a personal fortune of $50 billion, Gates has the resources to give his favorite solutions a major boost.

Jeff Goodell

在最近幾年，美國最富有的人開始專注於處理能源問題，投資百萬美元於各項產品，從高性能電池到可以將空氣中的二氧化碳去除的機器。比爾·蓋茲有五百億的個人資產，對於這個他最愛的議題應該有能力有一番作為。

傑夫·古德爾

I assume we will have figured out a way to efficiently utilize solar energy and tied that to an efficient way to use nuclear energy in such a way that it doesn't pose a serious environmental issue.

John Hickenlooper

我相信我們會找出有效運用太陽能的方法，而且將這個方法與有效使用核能相結合，讓核能不會對對環境造成嚴重問題。

約翰·赫根路柏

The U.S. now imports over half of its oil supply from the Middle East. This dangerous dependence on foreign energy sources is an issue of national security.

Kenny Marchant

現在美國有一半的石油是由中東進口的，這樣對外國能源的依賴很危險，攸關國家安全。

肯尼·馬爾查特

For me, it's my great honour that many people use blue LEDs or LED lightings now. So, we can contribute to the energy savings for the humans, so I'm very, very happy to contribute to the energy saving issues.

Hiroshi Amano

對我來說，現在很多人使用藍光 LED，也就是能發出藍光的 LED（發光二極體）燈，是我極大的榮耀。所以，我們能夠幫人們節約能源，我非常非常高興可以對節能做出貢獻。

天野浩

Unit 5　Environmental Protection
環境保護

1. Dialogue 實境對話　　6-5

A: Have you heard of "Fly, Kite Fly"?

B: No, what is it?

A: It's a documentary film about eagles in Taiwan.

B: I'm not sure if I would want to buy a ticket to watch a film about eagles in the movie theater.

A: This documentary film is about more than eagles; it focuses on environmental protection.

B: Are eagles good for the environment?

A: Yes, they can help agriculture by catching rats which live on farms and spread contagious diseases.

B: Then farmers must love having eagles flying around their farms.

A: The pesticides and rat poisons that farmers currently use have killed huge numbers of eagles.

B: How serious is the situation?

A: At the moment, only about 300 eagles still exist in Taiwan. In conclusion, eagles are in danger of extinction.

B: What can be done about it?

A: Most important of all is to promote friendly agriculture.

B: You mean not using pesticides and rat poisons?

A: That's right.

B: But it would cost too much for the farmers, and consumers might not want to pay high prices.

A: That's precisely why they should watch the documentary film and be educated about the serious problem.

中文翻譯

A： 你聽過「老鷹想飛」嗎？

B： 沒聽過，那是什麼？

A： 那是一部關於台灣老鷹的紀錄片。

B： 我不可能會想要買電影票進場去看一部關於老鷹的電影。

A： 這部紀錄片不只是關於老鷹，重點在於環境保護。

B： 老鷹對環境有利嗎？

A： 是的，老鷹對農業有幫助，因為他們能抓農場上會播傳染病的老鼠。

B： 那麼農人一定會很喜歡有老鷹在他們農場附近飛翔。

A： 現在農人使用的殺蟲劑和捕鼠毒物導致了大量老鷹死亡。

B： 情況有多嚴重？

A： 現在台灣僅存約三百隻老鷹，總而言之，老鷹瀕臨絕種。

B： 我們可以做什麼來改善這個情形呢？

A： 最重要的是提倡友善農業。

B： 你的意思是不要使用殺蟲劑和捕鼠毒物嗎？

A： 你說的對。

B： 但是這樣農人會要花很多錢，消費者不太可能會願意付高昂的價格。

A： 就因為如此更該看這部紀錄片，學習這個嚴重問題的相關事項。

字彙與片語

- documentary [ˌdɑkjəˈmɛntərɪ] a. （電影、電視等）記錄的；記實的
- spread [sprɛd] v. 傳播
- contagious [kənˈtedʒəs] a. 接觸傳染性的
- pesticide [ˈpɛstɪˌsaɪd] n. 殺蟲劑
- extinction [ɪkˈstɪŋkʃən] n. 絕種

2. Article 文章

Environmental Impacts of Different Forms of Energy

The most frequent forms of energy used today include coal, natural gas and nuclear power. There are also renewable energy sources, like wind power and solar energy. Each of them has its negative environmental consequences, which cannot be solved in the near future.

Coal is heavily used in countries like China and India, where coal power plants are built without the implementation of government regulations. The biggest impact of coal is carbon dioxide emissions. Natural gas also produces CO_2 emissions. It's time for industries to participate in the debates on how to reduce the scale of emissions in order to control global warming. Nuclear power plants have serious problems with waste disposal and they use too much water. Furthermore, the biggest concern for local residents is the safety issues of nuclear power plants. With renewable energy, the environmental impacts still exist. For example, wind power takes a lot of land use and produces a lot of noise, and wind turbines do terrible damage to birds. Solar energy is clean but extremely expensive for every household to employ. All too often, one has to pay more for green energy, such as solar panels.

As seen from the above, real eco-friendly energy is not yet easily available to everyone on earth. Developed countries are concerned that developing countries do not reduce their CO_2 emissions because of economic reasons. Environmental consequences of energy have often become political issues in the international economic forums.

不同形式的能源對環境的衝擊

現今最常使用的能源形式包含有煤、天然瓦斯、核能，還有再生能源的來源，例如風力發電與太陽能，每一種都有對環境負面的影響，短時間無法解決。

中國與印度等國家非常仰賴煤礦，在那裡火力發電廠經常不依照政府法規而建造，煤產生最大的衝擊是二氧化碳的排放，天然氣也會製造二氧化碳，現在產業該來參與討論要如何減低排放量，才能控制全球暖化。核能發電廠的廢料造成了嚴重問題，消耗過多的水，還有最令當地居民感到不安的是核能發電廠的安全問題。再生能源對環境還是會造成問題，例如，風力發電需要大量的土地，會製造很大的噪音，風力渦輪對鳥類會造成很大傷害。太陽能非常環保，但是對於住家來說極為昂貴，綠能通常都需要很高的費用，例如太陽能板。

以上可知，真正環保的能源對世上一般人並不易獲得。已開發國家非常憂心，開發中國家因為經濟因素無法減少二氧化碳的排放量，能源對環境的影響經常成為國際經濟論壇的政治議題。

字彙與片語

* consequence ['kɑnsəˌkwɛns] n. 結果，後果
* implementation [ˌɪmpləmɛn'teʃən] n. 實施；實踐；執行

- carbon dioxide 二氧化碳
- scale [skel] n. 大小；規模
- disposal [dɪ'spoz!] n. 處理，處置
- forum ['forəm] n. 討論會

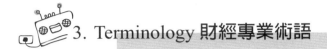

3. Terminology 財經專業術語

sustainability　永續性

　　永續性從廣義上來講，是能夠保持一定的過程或狀態，但這一詞普遍常用於研究生態和社會的關係。在生態方面，永續發展可以被界定為具能力的生態系統，能自我維持一切生態的過程、功能、生物多樣性、未來的生命力。

Ecology　生態學

　　是一門研究生物與其環境之間的相互關係的科學，由於與人類生存與發展的緊密相關而產生了多個生態學的研究熱點，如生物多樣性的研究、全球氣候變遷的研究、受損生態系的恢復與重建研究、永續發展研究等。

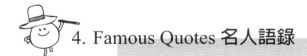

4. Famous Quotes 名人語錄

Climate change, demographics, water, food, energy, global health, women's empowerment – these issues are all intertwined. We cannot look at one strand in isolation. Instead, we must examine how these strands are woven together.

Ban Ki-moon

氣候變遷、人口統計資料、水、食品、能源、全球健康、婦女平權——這些議題彼此間都是關係密切的，我們不能只將一個問題獨立分開來談，相反的，我們必須要看這些議題如何互相影響。

潘基文

....

We learned that economic growth and environmental protection can and should go hand in hand.

Christopher Dodd

這一點我們已經明白了，經濟成長和環境保護可以同時並進，也必須同時並進。

克里斯多夫·多得

....

I tell my environmental friends that they have won. Every issue we look at from an energy perspective is now also looked at from an environmental perspective.

Joe Barton

我告訴我的環保朋友說他們贏了，每個我們從能源的觀點來看的議題，現在也都成為環保議題。

喬‧巴爾頓

. . . .

Environmental protection doesn't happen in a vacuum. You can't separate the impact on the environment from the impact on our families and communities.

Jim Clyburn

環境保護不會發生於孤立狀態，你無法將對環境的影響與對家庭與社區的影響分開來談。

吉米‧克萊柏恩

. . . .

But, as environment minister, I am very interested in a thriving German automobile industry, because I can only pay for the rising costs of environmental protection at home and abroad if there are people in Germany with jobs and who pay taxes.

Sigmar Gabriel

但是，身為環保部長，我對於德國的汽車業如此繁榮感到非常有興趣，因為我只有在德國有薪階級繳稅的情形下，才能繼續付為了保護國內外的環境所需要的日益高漲的費用。

斯格馬爾‧加柏里爾

Collaboration with Government
與政府合作

1. Dialogue 實境對話

 6-6

A: Would you take up that project suggested by the Ministry of Education?

B: That commissioned project of training interpreters seems to be interesting, but I would prefer not accepting it. I have had bad experiences working with the government.

A: Tell me more.

B: In short, everyone takes it for granted if you do a good job because of the public funds and resources. If there are some small problems, you become the target of public criticism.

A: I see what you mean. Above all, the first question they will raise is how and why you got the project.

B: That question came to mind when I first heard of the offer, too.

A: Perhaps they simply could not find any other language institutes that offer excellent interpretation training programs. We are outstanding in this field.

B: I know what we are good at, but we have our priorities in accepting offers.

A: What can we gain from offering training programs for beginning interpreters?

B: Maybe that can help spread a good reputation for our language institute?

A: So, have you decided to accept this project and work with the Ministry of Education?

B: Not yet. I need a few days to think thoroughly about this issue before I can make the right decision.

中文翻譯

A：你會接受教育部提出的那個專案嗎？

B：那個訓練口譯員的委託專案似乎很有意思，但是我不是很想接，我跟政府合作的經驗一直都很差。

A：告訴我發生了什麼事。

B：總而言之，如果你做得好，大家都視為理所當然，因為有公共資金與資源；但是如果發生了些小問題，你就成為了眾矢之的。

A：我知道你的意思，他們特別會提出的第一個問題是，你如何得到這個專案？為什麼是你得到？

B：我剛聽到那個提案時，也在想那個問題。

A：他們或許就是不能找到其它能提供優良口譯訓練計劃的語言中心，而我們是這個領域的翹楚。

B：我知道我們的長處，但是我們在接受提案是有優先順序的。

A：我們可以從提供口譯初學者的訓練計劃當中得到什麼？

B： 或許可以幫我們語言中心散播優良名聲？

A： 那麼，你決定好了接受這個專案，和教育部合作了嗎？

B： 還沒，我需要好好想幾天，才能做出正確的決定。

字彙與片語

- commissioned [kəˈmɪʃənd] a. 受委任的
- in short 總而言之，簡而言之
- take it for granted 視為理所當然
- priority [praɪˈɔrətɪ] n. 優先，重點；優先權
- thoroughly [ˈθɝolɪ] adv. 徹底地；認真仔細地

Collaboration with Government

In the past, private businesses expected the government to take charge of social issues, like environmental protection and helping the needy. In the time of economic uncertainty, business owners focused especially on the pressing competition and their own interests. In recent years, many businesses find it completely impossible to ignore the social needs and to not collaborate with the government.

All too often, we hear scandals involving companies with renowned brands, such as VW. After the auto company was caught cheating by adjusting the software for testing gas emissions, the reputation and image of the company experienced an unprecedented crisis. This scandal showed that the famous German car company has put its own economic interest far before social objective. Furthermore, because VW cars and car owners are all around the world, the serious damage it has done to the environment is borderless.

As we can see from the above, it is not enough only to have plans of corporate social responsibility but sustainability of social objectives should be part of the core of the entire business. Society appreciates a company with such a vision. For example, many customers are willing to pay more for products that are environmentally friendly, and governments reward green industries.

Private businesses can be enhanced by government and civil society alike. Collaboration with the government on health campaigns or joint projects can be prosperous and even desirable for entrepreneurs.

本文翻譯

與政府合作

以往私人企業期待政府負責處理社會議題，例如環境保護與幫助弱勢者。在經濟不穩定時，業主特別聚焦於激烈的競爭與自身的利益。最近幾年來，很多企業發現，不理會社會需要且不與政府合作是完全不可行的。

我們經常聽到知名品牌公司涉及醜聞，例如福斯汽車。在這家汽車公司測試排碳量的軟體被抓到造假後，公司的聲望與形象經歷了前所未聞的危機。這個醜聞顯示出這家知名汽車公司將自身經濟利益放在社會目的之前，還有，因為福斯汽車與車主遍及世界各地，對環境所造成的嚴重傷害是無邊際的。

如以上所述，只有企業社會責任計劃是不夠的，社會目標之永續性必須要是整個企業核心的一部分，社會看重有這種願景的公司。例如，很多消費者願意付較高的錢來買環保產品，而政府獎勵綠色產業。

私人企業的價值能夠被政府以及公民社會提高，與政府合作舉辦健康宣導活動或進行合作專案，對於企業家來說是很有前景，甚至是被看好的。

- collaboration [kə͵læbə'reʃən] n. 合作
- take charge of 負責；管理
- pressing ['prɛsɪŋ] a. 緊迫的，迫切的
- unprecedented [ʌn'prɛsə͵dɛntɪd] a. 無先例的，空前的
- desirable [dɪ'zaɪrəb!] a. 值得擁有的；令人滿意的

3. Terminology 財經專業術語

bidding　招標

　　招標是一種市場上尋找商業對象的行為，在一定範圍內公開貨物、服務、採購、工程的條件和要求，並邀請眾多投標人參加投標，之後按照原先規定程序，從中選擇合適者作為交易對象。

privatization 民營化

　　也稱為私有化，是指將國有企業的所有權轉給私人。近年來，一些以往由政府提供的服務，如教育、衛生等事業，在許多國家成為私有化最熱門的新對象。理論上，私有化有利於建立自由市場，鼓勵競爭，其支持者認為，私有化的這一特點使公眾以競爭性的價格獲得更廣泛的選擇，但是社會主義者反對國有企業的民營化。

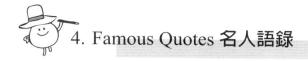
Government is the people's business and every man, woman and child becomes a shareholder with the first penny of tax paid.

Ronald Reagan

政府是全民的企業，所有男士、女士，還有小孩，一旦繳了第一分錢的稅後，就變成了股東了。

隆納 · 雷根

What is good about the United States is the sense that you can disagree with the government and not be seen as unpatriotic, although many in the government will try to make you seem unpatriotic.

George Mitchell

美國的優點是你可以不同意政府的看法，但是仍然不會被視作不愛國，雖然很多政府內的人會試著使你看起來似乎不愛國。

喬治 · 米薛爾

The digital revolution has deepened the crisis within representative democracy. But as it forces its demise, it might also dictate its future. Traditional representative democracy within nations is no longer enough. People want more participation and collaboration with their government.

Eduardo Paes

數位革命使得代議民主的危機更為嚴重，但是就如同數位革命迫使代議民主崩解，數位革命也左右了代議民主的未來，各國的傳統代議民主將會不敷使用，人們會更想要參與政府，與政府合作。

艾多爾 · 多帕耶斯

....

Companies should be able to share specific threat information with the government without the prospect of lawsuits hanging over their head.

Leon Panetta

企業應該要能夠與政府分享特定的威脅性資訊，而不用冒著會被告的危險。

黎昂 · 帕內塔

Corporate Social Responsibilities
企業的社會責任

 1. Dialogue 實境對話 6-7

A: Read this report of shoe donation to Africa. It's really very special and touching.

B: Why is it special? Haven't you heard that entrepreneurs around the world are doing charity work?

A: This shoe business owner came up with the idea that if you buy one pair of shoes from them, one pair of shoes will be donated to a kid in Africa by the company.

B: That's ingenious. Can the company still make profits?

A: Many customers bought shoes from the company and also advocated for the campaign. According to the report, they are making great profits.

B: Most entrepreneurs can only contribute to local charity work, but this campaign makes people in the world aware of the poverty issues in Africa and creates a good reputation of their own shoe company.

A: It's not like some other cases, in which people are not sure where their money donations are spent.

B: Since you have so many shoes, I suggest that you donate some of them to the poor here first.

A: After that, then I can sign up for this "Shoes for Africa" campaign.

中文翻譯

A： 你看一下這篇關於捐鞋給非洲的報導，真的非常特別又感人。

B： 有什麼特別？你沒有聽過世上有企業家在做慈善工作？

A： 這個鞋業業主想到了一個點子：如果你向他們買一雙鞋，他們公司就會捐一雙鞋給非洲的一個孩童。

B： 真是聰明。他們公司仍然可以獲利嗎？

A： 很多顧客向他們公司買鞋，也到處宣傳這個活動。根據這篇報導，他們獲利很高。

B： 大部分的企業家只能夠對地方的慈善工作有貢獻，但是這個活動使得全世界的人都認識到非洲貧窮的問題，也為他們自己的製鞋公司建立了好名聲。

A： 不像有的其它情形，捐款者不清楚所捐的錢的流向。

B： 既然你有那麼多鞋，我建議你先捐一些鞋給這裡的窮人。

A： 然後我就可以登記參加這個「捐鞋給非洲」的活動了。

- touching [ˈtʌtʃɪŋ] a. 動人的，感人的；令人同情的

- charity [ˈtʃærətɪ] n. 慈悲，博愛；慈善

- ingenious [ɪnˈdʒinjəs] a. 別出心裁的；足智多謀的

- advocate [ˈædvəkɪt] v. 擁護；提倡；支持

- poverty [ˈpɑvɚtɪ] n. 貧窮，貧困

Corporate Social Responsibilities

More and more corporations are participating in causes for the good of society. Multinational companies are interacting with local people by hosting joint campaigns with the local government. Companies which take corporate social responsibility can not only contribute to the well-being of society but also promote brands or businesses.

Environmental protection often receives a lot of attention in corporate social campaigns. Hardly any industry these days is not related to pollution or energy issues. Green businesses frequently campaign for the awareness of conservation and energy saving. Car and other auto industries, on the other hand, highlight how few emissions are caused by their vehicles. The food industry promotes organic farming and vegetation with no pesticides.

Donations to charity organizations have been trendier than ever. Some companies would rather donate things, such as clothing and shoes, than putting in money; some NGOs provide platforms for teaching kids in rural areas or selling products made by people with disabilities. Events on special social occasions, such as Christmas, can boost the participation of corporate social charity work.

Of course, discerning individuals are encouraged to take part in all corporate social activities. One thing to keep in mind is to distinguish the good companies from not-so-good ones. Doing some research ahead is always a good strategy to learn more about corporate cultures.

企業社會責任

　　越來越多企業參與社會福利活動，跨國公司常靠與當地政府合辦宣傳活動來達到與當地人的互動，負擔企業社會責任的公司不但能對社會福祉有貢獻，也可以宣傳品牌或企業。

　　環境保護經常為社會宣傳活動關注的一大焦點，現在幾乎沒有任何工業與汙染或能源議題無關。綠能產業通常宣導要注意節約能源。而小客車與其它汽車產業則強調他們交通工具排放廢氣之少；食品產業宣導不用殺蟲劑的有機農業與耕種。

　　捐錢給慈善機構變得非常流行，有些公司比較不喜歡捐錢，相較而言，他們比較喜歡捐像是衣物與鞋子的物資。有些非營利組織提供平台，用來提供偏鄉地區的孩童教育，或是賣身心障礙者的作品。特別節慶的活動，例如聖誕節，可以使參與企業社會慈善活動的人數增加。

　　當然，企業社會活動會鼓勵明智的個人來參與。有一點要記住的是，要能分辨好公司與不甚好的公司，事前做些功課總是個學習企業文化的好策略。

字彙與片語

- cause [kɔz] n. 原因;起因
- hardly ['hɑrdlɪ] adv. 幾乎不,簡直不
- awareness [ə'wɛrnɪs] n. 察覺;覺悟;體認
- lighlight ['haɪˌlaɪt] v. 使顯著;強調
- discerning [dɪ'zɝnɪŋ] a. 有識別力的;眼光敏銳的
- distinguish [dɪ'stɪŋgwɪʃ] v. 區別;識別

3. Terminology 財經專業術語

corporate social responsibilities 企業的社會責任

企業社會責任並無公認定義,但一般泛指企業超越道德、法律、公眾要求的標準,於進行商業活動時亦考慮到對各相關利益者造成的影響。企業社會責任的概念是基於商業運作必須符合可持續發展的想法,企業除了考慮自身的財政和經營狀況外,也要加入其對社會和自然環境所造成的影響的考量。

charitable activity 公益活動

公益活動是企業贊助和支持某項社會公益事業的公共關係實務活動,特別是指一些經濟效益比較好的企業,用來擴大影響,提高名聲的重要手段,例如,服裝公司為體操團贊助服裝,飲料廠為育幼院贊助飲料等等。

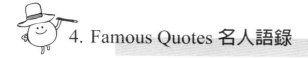

Companies should not have a singular view of profitability. There needs to be a balance between commerce and social responsibility. The companies that are authentic about it will wind up as the companies that make more money.

Howard Schultz

企業不應該只有一種獲利的看法，他們需要在商業與社會責任之間求得某種平衡，眞正如此做的企業最終會能賺更多錢。

霍華德・舒茲

· ·

I believe in trying to get a balance between individual freedom on the one hand and social responsibility on the other.

Chris Patten

我相信我們該要在個人自由與社會責任兩者之間求得某種平衡。

克里斯・帕特恩

· ·

The voluntary approach to corporate social responsibility has failed in many cases.

David Suzuki

很多企業主動參與社會責任的作法都失敗了。

大衛・鈴木

Successful people have a social responsibility to make the world a better place and not just take from it.

Carrie Underwood

成功者有社會責任使這個世界變得更好，而不是只是一味從社會中獲利。

凱利 · 恩德伍迪

....

There are writers who say they have no social responsibility except to write a good book, but that doesn't satisfy me.

Sheri Stewart Tepper

有些作家聲稱他們除了寫好書之外，沒有任何社會責任，但是我對這樣的說法並不滿意。

雪莉 · 史都華 · 特派爾

Chapter 7 Case Studies
個案研究

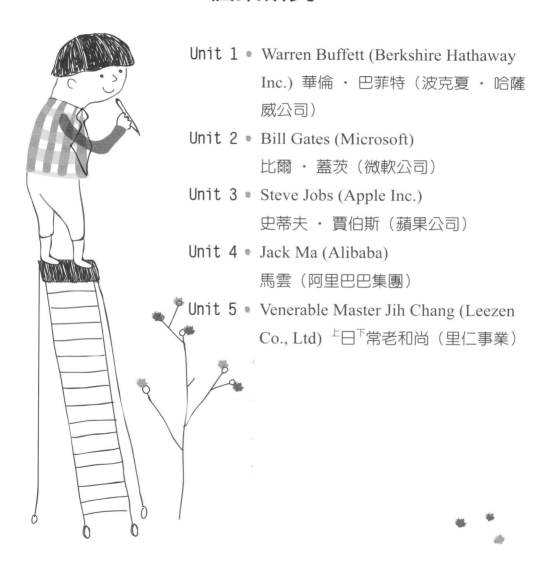

Unit 1　Warren Buffett (Berkshire Hathaway Inc.) 華倫・巴菲特（波克夏・哈薩威公司）

1. Warren Buffett 華倫・巴菲特

Warren Buffett was born in Omaha, Nebraska, the United States in 1930. He is often referred to as the "Oracle of Omaha" or "Sage of Omaha" and is internationally regarded as an exceptionally successful investor, especially in the area of stocks. Buffett is the chairman, president and CEO of Berkshire Hathaway, managing holdings in newspaper publishing, manufacture, energy, insurance, food and beverage industries, etc. Buffett has been ranked as one of the world's top wealthiest people. He is also widely known for his philanthropic endeavors and is very influential for both his opinions on investment and his world's view.

華倫・巴菲特在 1930 年生於美國內布拉斯加州的奧馬哈，他常被稱為「奧馬哈的聖人」或「奧馬哈的賢者」，國際公認為非常成功的投資家，特別是在股票方面。巴菲特是波克夏・哈薩威公司的董事長、總裁、執行長，所經營的股票涵蓋報紙出版業、製造業、能源業、保險業、餐飲業等等。巴菲特是世界上最富有的人之一，他以從事慈善事業而聞名，他的投資觀點與世界觀都非常有影響力。

2.Berkshire Hathaway Inc. 波克夏 · 哈薩威公司

Berkshire Hathaway Inc. is an American multinational conglomerate holding company headquartered in Omaha, Nebraska, United States. Under Warren Buffett's leadership, the company has become immensely successful. In the beginning, Buffett focused on buying long-term stock holdings, but later on, he more often simply purchased the entire companies. Berkshire Hathaway now owns a wide diversity of businesses, including assets in media (The Washington Post), insurance (GEICO), oil (Exxon), etc. After the company's significant investment in Coca-Cola, Buffett became director of the soft drink company from 1989 until 2006. Buffett has also served as director of Citigroup Global Markets Holdings, Graham Holdings Company and The Gillette Company. According to the Forbes Global 2000 list and formula, Berkshire Hathaway is the fifth largest public company in the world.

波克夏 · 哈薩威公司是個美國跨國控股事業企業集團,總部位於美國內布拉斯加州的奧馬哈,在華倫 · 巴菲特的領導下,這家公司經營得非常成功。在初期,巴菲特主要是買長期的股票,但是之後他經常買下整家公司,波克夏 · 哈薩威公司現今擁有的業務非常多元化,包含媒體(華盛頓時報)、保險(蓋可公司)、石油(埃克森石油公司)等等。在大幅投資於可口可樂後,巴菲特擔任可口可樂 1989 年至 2006 年的理事長,巴菲特也擔任了花旗國際市場控股公司、葛拉漢控股公司、吉列公司的理事長。根據富比仕 2000 年的排行表和計算方式，波克夏‧哈薩威公司是全世界第五大上市公司。

請參見 Berkshire Hathaway Inc. 官網 http://www.berkshirehathaway.com/

3. Buffett's Famous Quotes 巴菲特語錄

"Price is what you pay. Value is what you get."

「你付出的是價錢，得到的是價值。」

....

"Be fearful when others are greedy and greedy when others are fearful."

「別人貪婪時，你要恐懼；別人恐懼時，你要貪婪。」

....

"Shares are not mere pieces of paper. They represent part ownership of a business. So, when contemplating an investment, think like a prospective owner."

「股票不是紙張，他們代表對一家企業的部分擁有權，所以在考慮投資時，要將自己視為未來的公司所有人。」

....

"All there is to investing is picking good stocks at good times and staying with them as long as they remain good companies."

「投資不過就是在好時機時挑對股票，只要他們的公司運作保持良好，就保有這些股票。」

....

"The basic ideas of investing are to look at stocks as business, use the market's fluctuations to your advantage, and seek a margin of safety. That's what Ben Graham taught us. A hundred years from now they will still be the cornerstones of investing."

「投資最基礎的便是要將股票視爲企業，利用市場的波動，尋找安全利潤，這是班・葛拉漢教我們的，從現在起的一百年後還會是投資的基礎。」

....

"If, when making a stock investment, you're not considering holding it at least ten years, don't waste more than ten minutes considering it."

「在投資股票時，如果你不會想要至少十年擁有這張股票，那麼就不要浪費多於十分鐘考慮買下。」

....

"If you own your stocks as an investment — just like you'd own an apartment, house or a farm — look at them as a business."

「將你所擁有股票視爲投資——就像你擁有公寓、房子、農場那樣，將他們視爲事業。」

....

"The difference between successful people and really successful people is that really successful people say no to almost everything."

「成功者與真正成功者的分別在於，真正成功者會拒絕幾乎所有的事情。」

. . . .

"Invest in as much of yourself as you can, you are your own biggest asset by far."

「盡最大能力投資你自己，你是你自己最大的資產。」

. . . .

"I tell college students, when you get to be my age you will be successful if the people who you hope to have loved you, do love you."

「我告訴大學的學子，當你到了我這個年紀，如果你希望的那些愛你的人，是真的愛你的，你就可以算是個成功的人了。」

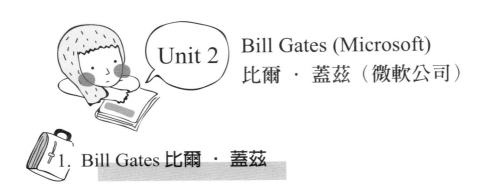

Unit 2　Bill Gates (Microsoft)
比爾・蓋茲（微軟公司）

1. Bill Gates 比爾・蓋茲

　　Bill Gates was born in Seattle, Washington, the United States in 1955. He is an extremely famous and successful computer programmer and entrepreneur. In 1975, Gates and partner Paul Allen built the world's largest software company, Microsoft. Gates is widely considered the innovative leader in the personal computer revolution. Despite the fact that his business tactics are often criticized, Microsoft has become a great success. Gates has become the world's wealthiest person. Through the Bill & Melinda Gates Foundation, which was established in 2000, Gates has launched many various charitable projects around the world for philanthropic causes.

　　比爾・蓋茲在 1955 年生於美國華盛頓州的西雅圖，他是位極著名且成功的電腦程式設計師與創業家。他在 1975 年與保羅・艾倫成立了全世界最大的軟體公司：微軟公司。蓋茲被公認為是個人電腦革命的創新領導者，即使他的商業手段經常受人批評，微軟公司還是非常成功，蓋茲成為世界首富。透過成立於 2000 年的比爾與梅琳達・蓋茨基金會，蓋茲推動了許多全球慈善事業。

2. Microsoft 微軟公司

Microsoft Corporation is an American multinational technology company headquartered in Redmond, Washington. It was founded in 1975 and is the worldwide leader in computer software, services, devices and solutions. Its mission is to help people and businesses achieve more and realize their full potential. Its best known software products are the Microsoft Windows line of operating systems, Microsoft Office office suite, and Internet Explorer web browsers. Microsoft is the biggest software platform producer and one of the most valuable companies in the world.

微軟公司是一家美國跨國的科技公司，總部設在華盛頓州的瑞得蒙，成立於 1975 年，是全世界在電腦軟體、服務、設備、解決方案的業界翹楚。公司的使命是要幫助個人和公司達成更多任務，實現最高潛能。最出名的軟體有作業系統的微軟 Windows、Office，還有瀏覽器 Internet Explorer。微軟是世界最大軟體平台的生產公司，也是世上市值最高的公司之一。

請參見 microsoft 官網 http://www.microsoft.com/

3. Gates's Famous Quotes 蓋茲語錄

"Patience is a key element of success."

「耐心是成功的關鍵要素。」

....

"Success is a lousy teacher. It seduces smart people into thinking they can't lose."

「成功是位很差勁的老師，會讓聰明的人誤以爲他們不會失敗。」

....

"It's fine to celebrate success, but it is more important to heed the lessons of failure."

「我們可以慶祝成功，但是更重要的是要注意失敗的教訓。」

....

"Life is not fair — get used to it."

「人生而不平等——接受這個事實吧。」

....

"To win big, you sometimes have to take big risks."

「要想大贏，你有時必須要冒大風險。」

....

"I choose a lazy person to do a hard job because a lazy person will find an easy way to do it."

「我會選個懶惰的人來做苦差事，因為懶人會去找容易的方法來
達成任務。」

....

"Don't compare yourself with anyone in this world. If you do so,
you are insulting yourself."

「不要把你自己與世上其他人做比較，如果你去做比較，就是在
汙辱自己。」

....

"As we look ahead into the next century, leaders will be those who
empower others."

「我們看看下個世紀，領導者會是可以賦予他人力量的人。」

....

"I really had a lot of dreams when I was a kid, and I think a great
deal of that grew out of the fact that I had a chance to read a lot."

「童年時我真的有很多夢想，我認為這是和我有機會大量閱讀有
很大關係。」

....

"Your most unhappy customers are your greatest source of learning."

「對你最不滿意的客戶是你學習的最大來源所在。」

....

"This is a fantastic time to be entering the business world, because business is going to change more in the next 10 years than it has in the last 50."

「現在是進入商場的良好時機，因為接下來的十年內，商業將會發生比過去五十年中還要多的變化。」

....

"The vision is really about empowering workers giving them all the information about what's going on so they can do a lot more than they've done in the past."

「願景真的就是讓員工獲得力量，讓他們知道周遭發生的一切，他們才能夠做出比過去還要多很多的事情。」

....

"I failed in some subjects in exam, but my friend passed in all. Now he is an engineer in Microsoft and I am the owner of Microsoft."

「我有幾科被當掉了，但是我的朋友都通過了，現在他是微軟的工程師，我是微軟的老闆。」

....

"Technology is just a tool. In terms of getting the kids working together and motivating them, the teacher is the most important."

「科技只是工具，至於讓小孩子一起合作，激勵他們，老師才是最重要的。」

....

"If you think your teacher is tough, wait till you get a boss."

「如果你認為你的老師很嚴厲，等到你有了老闆再看看。」

Unit 3　Steve Jobs (Apple Inc.)
史蒂夫・賈伯斯（蘋果公司）

1. Steve Jobs 史蒂夫・賈伯斯

Steve Jobs (February 24, 1955 - October 5, 2011) was a world famous American information technology entrepreneur. He was the co-founder, chairman and chief executive officer (CEO) of Apple Inc. Jobs is widely recognized as a pioneer of the microcomputer revolution of the 1970s; he and Steve Wozniak co-founded Apple in 1976. Apple's ingenious products, which include the iPod, iPhone, iPad, etc, are now seen as dictating the evolution of modern technology. Steve Jobs was highly praised for his stylish designs and brand marketing. After battling pancreatic cancer for nearly a decade, Jobs died in Palo Alto on October 5, 2011. He was 56 years old. Shortly after his death, Jobs's official biographer, Walter Isaacson, described him as a "creative entrepreneur whose passion for perfection and ferocious drive revolutionized six industries: personal computers, animated movies, music, phones, tablet computing, and digital publishing."

史蒂夫・賈伯斯（生於 1955 年 2 月 24 日，2011 年 10 月 5 日逝世）為舉世聞名的美國科技創業家，他是蘋果公司的共同創辦者、董事長、執行長。賈伯斯為世人公認的 1970 年代微電腦革命先驅，他與史蒂夫・沃茲尼克共同創立了蘋果公司。蘋果公司設計精巧的產品，包含 iPod、iPhone、iPad 等等，一般公認，主導了現代科技。史蒂夫・賈伯斯充滿風格的設計和品牌行銷為人所稱道。賈柏斯在對抗胰腺癌幾近十年後，於 2011 年 10 月 5 日在帕羅奧多市逝世，享年 56 歲。在他過世後，賈伯斯的授權的傳記作家沃爾特・艾薩克森描述賈伯斯為「充滿創意的企業家，他追求完美的熱情與狂熱的魄力對以下六個領域產生革新性的影響：個人電腦、動畫電影、音樂、手機、平板電腦、電子出版。」

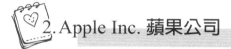

2. Apple Inc. 蘋果公司

Apple Inc. is an American multinational technology company based in Cupertino, California. Its hardware products include the iPhone smartphone, the iPad tablet computer, the Mac personal computer, the iPod portable media player, the Apple Watch smartwatch, and other devices. Aside from those products, Apple offers consumer computer software and online services as well. The products Apple has introduced to the world are innovative and revolutionary, and almost each newly released product has strongly influenced competitors. It is the world's largest information technology company by revenue and has zero debt. There are numerous Apple retail stores around the world.

蘋果公司為一家美國的跨國公司，位於加州的庫比蒂諾市，所生產的硬體產品包含智慧型手機 iPhone、平板電腦 iPad、Mac 個人電腦、iPod 可攜帶式的媒體播放器、智慧型手表 Apple Watch 等等。除了這些產品外，蘋果公司提供消費型電腦軟體，以及很多線上服務。蘋果公司所帶給世人的產品都充滿創新，具有革命性，而且幾乎所有新發表的產品都對競爭者產生很大的影響。以營利來說，蘋果公司為全世界最大的資訊科技公司，而且沒有任何虧損。目前在世界各地有非常多家的蘋果零售商店。

請參見 Apple 官網 http://www.apple.com/

3. Jobs's Famous Quotes 賈伯斯語錄

"I'm convinced that about half of what separates the successful entrepreneurs from the non-successful ones is pure perseverance."

「我深信成功與不成功的企業家的差別，有一半是堅忍。」

....

"That's been one of my mantras — focus and simplicity. Simple can be harder than complex; you have to work hard to get your thinking clean to make it simple."

「這是我的魔咒——聚焦和簡單，簡單可以比複雜還難；必須要努力才能使思想純淨、簡化想法。」

....

"My favorite things in life don't cost any money. It's really clear that the most precious resource we all have is time."

「我生命中最喜歡的事不用花任何錢。這真的顯而易見，我們所擁有的最珍貴資源是時間。」

....

"Innovation distinguishes between a leader and a follower."

「創新是領導者與追隨者的區別所在。」

....

"Sometimes when you innovate, you make mistakes. It is best to admit them quickly, and get on with improving your other innovations."

「有時候你在創新時會犯錯，最好馬上承認，然後繼續改進其它創新。」

....

"I'm as proud of many of the things we haven't done as the things we have done. Innovation is saying no to a thousand things."

「我對於很多我們沒有做的事情，感到與做了的事一樣驕傲，創新需要拒絕無數的事情。」

....

"Technology is nothing. What's important is that you have a faith in people, that they're basically good and smart, and if you give them tools, they'll do wonderful things with them."

「科技沒有什麼，重要的是要對人有信心，他們基本上都是善良且聰明，如果你給他們工具，他們會創造出美好的事物。」

....

"A lot of times, people don't know what they want until you show it to them."

　「很多時候人們需要你展示給他們看，才知道他們要的是什麼。」

⋯⋯⋯⋯⋯⋯⋯⋯⋯⋯⋯⋯⋯⋯⋯⋯⋯⋯⋯⋯⋯⋯⋯⋯⋯⋯⋯⋯⋯⋯⋯

"You can't just ask customers what they want and then try to give that to them. By the time you get it built, they'll want something new."

　「你不能光問消費者他們想要什麼，然後試圖滿足他們，等到你生產完成那樣東西，他們又會要別的新東西了。」

⋯⋯⋯⋯⋯⋯⋯⋯⋯⋯⋯⋯⋯⋯⋯⋯⋯⋯⋯⋯⋯⋯⋯⋯⋯⋯⋯⋯⋯⋯⋯

"You've got to start with the customer experience and work back toward the technology — not the other way around."

　「你必須要從使用者的經驗開始，然後再從科技下手——而不是反方向進行。」

⋯⋯⋯⋯⋯⋯⋯⋯⋯⋯⋯⋯⋯⋯⋯⋯⋯⋯⋯⋯⋯⋯⋯⋯⋯⋯⋯⋯⋯⋯⋯

"Your work is going to fill a large part of your life, and the only way to be truly satisfied is to do what you believe is great work. And the only way to do great work is to love what you do. If you haven't found it yet, keep looking. Don't settle. As with all matters of the heart, you'll know when you find it."

　「你的工作會占據生命的一大部分時間，唯一能對工作真正滿意的方法，便是要從事自認為偉大的工作，唯一能成就偉大事業的方法是要熱愛你的工作，如果你還沒找到這樣的工作，繼續尋找，不要妥協。就像所有與心很有關係的事一樣，一旦你找到了，就會知道。」

"Don't let the noise of others' opinions drown out your own inner voice."

「不要讓其他人的意見淹沒了你自己內心的聲音。」

"Stay hungry. Stay foolish."

「求知若飢，虛心若愚。」

"The greatest thing is when you do put your heart and soul into something over an extended period of time, and it is worth it."

「最偉大的莫過於長時間專心致力於某事，而且是值得的事情。」

"Being the richest man in the cemetery doesn't matter to me … Going to bed at night saying we've done something wonderful … that's what matters to me."

「當個墓園最有錢的人對我沒有任何意義……就寢前說我們已經做完了美好的事情……那才是對我有意義的事。」

Unit 4

Jack Ma (Alibaba)
馬雲（阿里巴巴集團）

1. Jack Ma 馬雲

Jack Ma (Chinese: 馬雲) was born in Hangzhou, Zhejiang Province, China in 1964. At an early age, he was very keen on learning English and Western culture. He would guide travelers around the city for free to practice English, and later on English has helped him in many ways. Jack Ma graduated from the Hangzhou Teacher's Institute with a bachelor's degree in English in 1988. He became a lecturer in English at the Hangzhou Dianzi University. In 1999, Jack Ma founded Alibaba, a China-based business-to-business marketplace platform. After the IPO in 2014, the Internet giant Alibaba made its market debut in the United States, and Jack Ma became China's richest person (Hong Kong not included). He is the first mainland Chinese entrepreneur to appear on the cover of Forbes. Alibaba is currently one of the biggest e-commerce technology firms in the world.

馬雲在 1964 年出生於中國的浙江省杭州市。在很年輕的時候，他就對學習英語和西方文化產生很大的興趣。他會義務提供導遊服務，以和遊客練習英語，後來英語對他在很多方面都有很大的助益。馬雲於 1988 年畢業於杭州師範學院外語系，獲得英語學士學位，之後於杭州電子工學院擔任英語教師。馬雲於 1999 年創立了阿里巴巴集團，那是一個位於中國，企業與企業間交易的平台。在 2014 年網路巨型公司阿里巴巴集團上市後，等同於在美國市場正式亮相，馬雲成為了全中國最富有的人（不包含香港在內），他也是第一位登上富比仕雜誌的中國大陸企業家。阿里巴巴集團目前為全世界最大的電子商務科技公司之一。

2. Alibaba 阿里巴巴集團

　　The Alibaba Group is a family of successful Internet-based businesses. Alibaba is China's largest online commerce company and one of the world's biggest online commerce companies. It has three main sites: Taobao, Tmall and Alibaba.com, and they all have hundreds of millions of users and host millions of businesses. Currently Alibaba provides consumer-to-consumer, business-to-consumer and business-to-business sales services via web portals. It also provides electronic payment services, a shopping search engine and data-centric cloud computing services. Eighty percent of China's online shopping market is dominated by Alibaba. Alibaba has become one of the most valuable tech-companies in the world after raising $25 billion from its U.S. IPO. It is also one of the most valuable Chinese public companies, ranking among some of China's state-owned enterprises.

　　阿里巴巴集團為一家成功的網路集團公司，是中國最大也是全世界最大的電子商務公司之一。它擁有三個主要領域：淘寶、Tmall、

Alibaba.com，他們都擁有無法計數的使用者，以及無數的公司。目前的阿里巴巴集團提供消費者對消費者、業者對消費者、業者對業者的網路銷售服務，同時也提供電子支付服務和購物搜尋引擎，還有數據為中心的雲端計算服務。百分之八十的中國電子購物市場為阿里巴巴集團所獨佔，阿里巴巴集團於美國一上市就獲得了 250 億美元。之後便成為世界上市值最高的科技公司之一，同時也是中國上市公司中市值最高的公司之一，可與一些中國國有企業相比。

請參見 Alibaba 官網 http://www.alibaba.com/

3. Jack Ma's Famous Quotes 馬雲語錄

「我們有一個理想，就像童話故事《阿里巴巴和四十大盜》一樣。阿里巴巴打開芝麻之門，讓更多人受益，獲得財富。」

"We have a vision: Ali Baba and the Forty Thieves. Alibaba will 'open sesame' so more people will benefit from the treasures."

....

「第一個想到的是你的客户，第二想到你的員工，其他才是想對手。」

"Put the customers first, the employees second, and the shareholders third."

....

「有一樣東西不能討價還價，就是企業文化、使命感與價值觀。」

"Corporate culture, missions and values cannot be bargained over."

....

「我覺得我們應該為結果付報酬，為過程鼓掌。」

"I think we should pay for the result and applaud for the process."

....

「貿易是一種自由，貿易是一種人權。貿易不應該被用來成為對抗其他國家的工具。」

Trade is a freedom. Trade is a human right. Trade should not be used as a tool against other nations.

....

「貿易不是關於交換貨品，貿易是文化、激情、創新和創造。」

Trading is not about trading products. Trading is about the culture, passion, innovation, and creation.

....

「一流高手是眼睛裡面沒有對手，所以我經常說我沒有對手，原因是我心中沒有對手。」

"There are no competitors in the eyes of the first-class player, so I often say I do not have competitors because I do not have competitors in my mind."

....

「心中有敵，天下皆爲你敵人；心中無敵，無敵於天下。」

"If there are enemies in your mind, all the people are your enemies; if there are no enemies in your mind, there are no real enemies in the world."

....

「一個公司在兩種情況下最容易犯錯誤，第一是有太多的錢的時候，第二是面對太多的機會。」

"A company is likely to make mistakes under two conditions: first is to have too much money, and the second is to have too many opportunities."

....

「網際網路是四乘一百米接力賽，你再厲害，也只能跑一棒，應該把機會給年輕人。」

"The Internet is like a relay race for 4x100 meters. No matter how good you are, you can only run for one relay and have to pass the opportunities to the younger people."

....

「一個創業者最重要的，也是你最大的財富，就是你的誠信。」

"The most important thing and the most precious wealth for an entrepreneur is integrity."

....

「創業者光有激情和創新是不夠的，它需要很好的體系、制度、團隊以及良好的盈利模式。」

"An entrepreneur should have not only passion and innovation but also sound systems, regulations, teams and management patterns."

....

「最核心的問題是根據市場去制定你的產品，關鍵是要傾聽客戶的聲音。」

"The core issue is to design your product according to the market. The key point is to listen to the customers' needs."

. . . .

「慈善必須以商業的計劃執行，以商業的形式執行，慈善才能走得久走得長。」

"Philanthropy has to be carried out with business strategies, in business styles, so that it can last longer."

. . . .

「今天很殘酷，明天更殘酷，後天很美好，但是大多數人死在明天晚上，看不到後天的太陽！」

"Today is hard, tomorrow will be worse, but the day after tomorrow will be sunshine. If you give up tomorrow, you will never see the sunshine."

Unit 5 Venerable Master Jih Chang (Leezen Co., Ltd)^上日^下常老和尚（里仁事業）

1. The Origin of Leezen Co. and its founder
里仁事業的成立緣起與創辦人

Nearly two decades ago, Venerable Master Jih Chang (1929-2004) started to promote organic farming against all odds with the mission to save the Earth from pollution by chemical pesticides and fertilizers and to care for all living beings. His ultimate aim was to safeguard and sustain the whole ecological environment. At the same time, he also noticed the widespread use of chemical additives in many food products and household goods, causing great damage to general health. In the year of 1998, Leezen Co. was thus established by his lay disciples, who were committed to "venturing into the forest no one dares to". With firm belief in the principle of integrity, Leezen insists on reciprocity rather than self-interest and collaboration instead of competition. A collaborative and trusting cycle has been formed among producers, vendors and consumers. To date, Leezen has grown to become a widely recognized and supported social enterprise.

^上日^下常老和尚（1929-2004 年）在二十多年前，為了挽救因農藥與化肥污染而受創的大地，關懷一切自然萬物與有情生命，排除萬難，大力倡導推動有機農耕，以維護永續生態環境；同時，老和尚也察覺到各項食品、用品中使用很多化學合成添加物，嚴重危害大眾健

康，於是由在家弟子於1998年成立里仁事業股份公司，決心要做「該做但還沒有人做的事」。里仁一向秉持「誠信」的理念，堅持「以互利取代自利，以合作化解競爭」，帶動生產者、銷售者、消費者三方彼此信賴的合作關係，至今已成為受到各界鼓勵支持的社會企業。

請參見 " 天天里仁 " https://www.leezen.com.tw/

2. Leezen Co., Ltd 里仁事業股份有限公司

Leezen recognizes that ultimate reward is in the pursuit of mutual benefits over self-interests; mutual gratitude, not profit-seeking competition, is the basis of lasting partnership. Leezen has always treated people and the Earth with this simple pure heart. Being mindful of organic farmers' hardships and needs for assistance, Leezen, in partnership with like-minded consumers, procures all organic produce farmers were capable of growing and harvesting.

To cherish each crop planted with no chemical pesticides and to motivate more people to treat the Earth right, Leezen closely collaborates with vendors to develop and manufacture a variety of health foods, household items and clothing made from organic cotton. Leezen encourages food manufacturers to use predominately local organic or natural ingredients for all food items, and to avoid using artificial flavors, colors, and preservatives to secure the natural taste of food. Leezen also promotes the use of materials that are biodegradable, eco-friendly and harmless to human health in order to minimize the impact to the environment.

Taking the role of channel, Leezen operates and adheres to the principle of win-win and integrity, and has successfully earned the trust of farmers, vendors and consumers alike. Leezen advocates that farmers should tend to the crops with due respect of the nature; vendors should produce products as they are intended for their personal use. In return, consumers should cherish the quality and safety in the food and honor the dedication of the farmers and suppliers. It has not been an easy journey without frustration and challenges, but because of the belief that grateful support is far better than fault-finding, a virtuous cycle of mutual help has come to fruition.

里仁相信最真實有感的好處，始終來自攜手互利而非自利；最靜美長遠的合作關係是彼此扶助感謝，而非成為相互逐利的競爭者。里仁靜守著這樣簡單的純心，對待人及土地。因為同感農友轉作有機的艱辛，里仁以契約種植來保障農友收入，並滿心喜樂接納轉型期蔬果，號召志同道合的消費者，以實質購買，一起陪伴農友度過掙扎糊口的轉作歲月。

為了珍惜每一株未施農藥化肥的盛產蔬果，並帶動更多人投入實踐友善大地的行動，里仁與廠商攜手合作，一次次突破技術瓶頸，開發出各種溫柔對待身體並好好善待土地的食品、生活用品及有機棉品。鼓勵食品廠商優先選用本土有機或天然食材，盡可能地「不添加」並減少業界習以為常的加工層次，完全拒絕人工香料、化學色素、合成防腐劑，坦誠分享食物天然真實的安心本味。同時也邀請用品廠商選用容易分解、減少危害的友善成分，盡量降低便利消費對大地形成的衝擊。

里仁以串聯上下游的通路角色，持續在農友、廠商和消費者之間分享溝通，促成相倚互信、相知相惜的夥伴關係。因為認同這樣共存共榮的理念，「誠信」便成為彼此長期支持下最自然的期待：農友像是疼惜子女般呵護樹草蟲鳥生態、廠商以家人自用的心情來產製每一項商品、消費者也珍惜栽種人及製作者費盡心力才產出的安心好物。努力的過程中，雖然一路上有重重挫折與困難，但是因為相信感恩相挺遠比指責追究更有力量，因而點亮串起了一個群策群力、真心互助的良善循環。

請參見 " 天天里仁 " https://www.leezen.com.tw/

3. 上日下常老和尚語錄

"The success of the common people is actually like baits, which taste good but will cost you your life." ("The Voice of Bliss & Wisdom", 68)

「世間人所謂的成功，實際上是魚餌，魚餌讓你覺得很好吃，最後卻是要你的命。」（福智之聲第 68 期）

. . . .

"When the like-minded people on the same mission are united, incredible power can be forged. At that time, it is important not to fight against others, but to improve oneself in order to help others." ("The Voice of Bliss & Wisdom", 68)

「一群理念相同的人結合起來，會形成一股不可思議的新力量，那時要把握住一個原則，不是與別人作對，而是要進一步提升自己，幫助別人。」（福智之聲第 68 期）

....

"Success depends on the environment, and the environment depends on the forces of a group of like-minded people." ("The Voice of Bliss & Wisdom", 80)

「成功要靠環境，環境要靠一群同心同願的人一起來推動。」（福智之聲第 80 期）

....

"When we have an idea and put it into practice, we might not achieve good results immediately, but in the process, we have gradually changed." ("The Voice of Bliss & Wisdom", 80)

「當我們有了理念並去實踐時，雖非立即就能產生很好的效果，但是我們已經慢慢轉變了！」（福智之聲第 80 期）

....

"Our eating habits have done direct damages to our health and have caused great economic loss. If we can change our eating habits, the whole environment, including the forces of violence will be changed." ("The Voice of Bliss & Wisdom", 89)

「我們的飲食習慣，已經造成健康的直接損害、經濟的最大損失，如果能夠改變過來，整個大環境，包括暴力傾向也會隨著改過來。」（福智之聲第 89 期）

....

"As we develop the right compassion, we not only accumulate for ourselves the best merits, but also cultivate a clean environment for everyone around us." ("The Voice of Bliss & Wisdom", 132)

「照著正確的慈心理念慢慢去推展的話，不但爲自己積下一份最好的善淨資糧，也爲周圍相關的人培植了一片善淨的園地。」（福智之聲第 132 期）

....

從一顆慈悲的心出發

國家圖書館出版品預行編目資料

經理人英文／張文娟著.
ーー初版. ーー臺北市：五南, 2016.10
　　面；　公分
ISBN 978-957-11-8823-2（平裝）

1.商業英文　2.讀本

805.18　　　　　　　　105016564

1X0A

經理人英文

作　　者 ― 張文娟

發 行 人 ― 楊榮川

總 編 輯 ― 王翠華

主　　編 ― 朱曉蘋

英文校對 ― Laura Carter

封面設計 ― 陳翰陞

出 版 者 ― 五南圖書出版股份有限公司

地　　址：106台北市大安區和平東路二段339號4樓

電　　話：(02)2705-5066　　傳　　真：(02)2706-6100

網　　址：http://www.wunan.com.tw

電子郵件：wunan@wunan.com.tw

劃撥帳號：01068953

戶　　名：五南圖書出版股份有限公司

法律顧問　林勝安律師事務所　林勝安律師

出版日期　2016年10月初版一刷

定　　價　新臺幣440元